THE FOOL OF LOVE

THE FOOL OF LOVE

by
James Lees-Milne

Robinson Publishing
London

First published by
Robinson Publishing
11 Shepherd House
Shepherd Street
London W1Y 7LD

Copyright © James Lees-Milne, 1990

ISBN 1 85487 066 1

Typeset by Selectmove Ltd., London
Printed and bound in Great Britain by
Mackays of Chatham PLC*, Chatham, Kent*

'The dupe of friendship, and the fool of love; have I not reason to hate and to despise myself?'
The Plain Speaker (1826), William Hazlitt

(1)

"WHY, you're English!" Rupert exclaimed, and the two creases across his forehead vanished.

"Nein, nein, natürlich bin Ich Deutsch," the prisoner replied.

"Aren't you ashamed? Isn't it awful to be German?"

Ernst, too subdued by years of internment to be either cross or amused, forced a wry smile, tossed his head and laughed. The boy's callow heart was as cold as the dewy grass.

"Does my mother employ you?" Rupert asked. Nearly three years ago two-thirds of the servants left Templeton in a body, not to be replaced. Only the very old remained. And here was a new and comparatively young man. Rupert had no brothers or sisters; not even first cousins. He had never invited a school friend to stay because his mother was too busy to cope with an extra boy. And his father of course was at the front.

"No, your mother doesn't employ me," the other answered in faultless English. "No one employs me. At home *I* employ hundreds." Rupert looked astounded. The man must be a liar. The boy turned on his heels, left the walled garden and strolled back to the house for breakfast. He did not notice the garish daffodils, their yellow trumpets like telephone speaking tubes, his mother's pride, and the delicate blue speedwell, his mother's bugbear, in the long couch-grass which used to be earth lightly raked.

"Rupert," she said while she struggled with a

1

spoonful of *Force*, a newly invented cereal made of cardboard shavings and rendered soggy by a dash of blue skimmed milk, "I won't be back from the hospital till latish this evening. So you must amuse yourself somehow. I suppose I can't expect you to do a little weeding, say, in the daffodil border? That would be too much like school, wouldn't it? On the other hand, if you felt inclined, dear. Poor Father on his last leave said that Dodds must no longer do any work in the flower garden. Only concentrate on the kitchen garden. Dig for victory and all that. It's more than he can manage on his own even with the help of one of the German prisoners from the camp."

"Is that who he is then?"

"You don't mean to say you've seen him already? What does he look like?"

"A thin man in a sort of grey uniform, confessed he was a Bosch. He wasn't the least ashamed either."

"He wouldn't be. It's a pretty pass . . . Huns in one's own back garden." She rose from her chair and pushed away with the palm of her delicate hand a plate containing a half-eaten slice of burnt toast and a dab of unnaturally bright margarine. "Rancid as usual," she said, screwing up her mouth. And then, "Good-bye, dear. Enjoy yourself and be good."

Mrs Fiennes-Templeton gave her son a sharp peck on the cheek, drew herself up to a greater height than became her, and stalked ungainly from the bleak dining-room. Clutching the door-handle she turned her head. "Just blow out the spirit lamp when you've finished your kedgeree, and you might give Pritchard a hand with the breakfast things."

Amy Fiennes-Templeton was an upright woman. It was part of her trouble. She had never shown overt feelings for a human being. Consequently no

2

one knew whether she had any to spare. Joshua her husband and Rupert hadn't a clue. The first had minded for twelve years before August 1914, when he went with the Grenadier Guards across the Channel and kicked the dust of matrimony from his feet at Dover, rejoicing. Rupert, having had no experience of parental affection in any demonstrable sense, did not mind the deprivation of something he had never enjoyed. The father was tolerant of, but incurious about, his son. The two had seldom met since the war began and Joshua never wrote to Rupert either at Christmas or for the boy's birthday. Amy would remember to buy him presents for these festivities on which she would scribble, "With love from Father". Joshua's negligence was not caused by dislike of his son, but by idleness. Nevertheless Rupert was pathetically proud of his father's D.S.O. He looked upon him as a patriot hero and whatever belonged to his father he regarded as his own, almost part of himself by prescriptive right; and he was resentful of its use by others, even his mother. Neither love nor lust had so much as touched a chord of his being to date. No girl or boy had yet reached the fringes of his heart.

Polishing off the kedgeree Rupert pondered how he was to pass the day, indeed the days? He would look for the bicycle he knew one of the footmen had left behind. It was rusting in the harness-room unclaimed since William had been slaughtered on the Somme. Meanwhile Rupert drained a last mouthful of coffee—it tasted of acorns—scooping his little finger round the bottom of the cup and sucking the saturated remains of rationed sugar.

The dining-room door opened. Pritchard walked in carrying an oblong, brightly polished silver tray. She was a middle-aged woman with a wide expressive mouth and smiling fish eyes magnified through gold-rimmed *pince-nez* with the thickest imaginable lenses. She still wore a starched blue uniform and snow-white apron tied behind in a full bow; and over wispy, greying hair a cap with blue streamers.

"Now then, Master Rupert, stir your stumps. There's a war on, you know."

Rupert loathed the war and resented any mention of it unless it reflected on his father's heroism. He never followed the news in the papers and was embarrassed by the long Roll of Honour printed daily on the front page of the *Morning Post*. Talk of the battles made him yawn.

"Now what did yer Mummy say you was to do?" Pritchard cast a reproachful glance at the flame of the spirit lamp, still bravely flickering.

"Oh, gosh, yes," and moving leisurely towards the side-board he extinguished the lamp with a full, wet blow. The strong, acrid smell of methylated spirit hung an invisible cloud over the remains of breakfast. Pritchard, preparatory to clearing away, put the silver tray on the little round table at which mother and son had been eating in the bow window. Rupert dashed across the room, threw his arms round Pritchard's waist, gave her a bear's hug and a kiss which knocked her cap askew and proceeded to dance with her on the worn carpet. Pritchard caught her heel in a tear, wobbled and collapsed, a heap of laughter into a sofa with Rupert on top of her. Shaking and convulsed she stood up, adjusted her cap while Rupert with a deft tug untied her apron strings. Boredom and mischief were his impulse. Nevertheless he was shot with a momentary pang of guilt. To prolong the charade he piled the used plates, silver coffee pot, milk jug, marmalade jar on the tray in a sort of wild, whirlwind movement—raising the tray perilously above his head and prancing like Salome to the side-board, which he likewise swept clear of dishes, and waltzing through the baize door into the pantry.

Pritchard collected herself and followed. "I've had enough of you," she said, still giggling. "Now run along. I don't want none of yer interference with my washing up."

Rupert let himself out of the back door and ambled across the cobbled yard to the harness-room the far side of the courtyard. William's bicycle was there right enough. Things always remained at Templeton. It was propped against the partitioned pitch-pine wall in exactly the same place where he saw it in the last holidays. With his jerseyed arm Rupert swept from the leather saddle a film of plaster which had fallen from the ceiling. He noticed how the left side of the saddle was worn lower than the right as though William had had one leg shorter than the other. Both tyres were flat. Turning the bike upside down, he detached the tyres with the spanner, kept in a little pouch dangling from the back of the saddle, ripped out the tubes, pumped air into them, passed them through a bucket of water, detected the tiny perforations by the bubbles and stuck patches across the perished bits. By the time he had oiled the chain and pedals, lowered the seat and tested the dilapidated machine on the drive, it was 1 o'clock. Pritchard rang the gong just as though for a house party before the war, instead of for one boy, just fifteen and undersized for his age.

He spent the afternoon cycling down the lanes and raising clouds of dust which blew into the hedges and rested upon the primroses and celandines. This recreation had palled by tea-time. Rupert wandered

5

down the weed-choked terraces until he found himself in the kitchen garden where he threw himself down on the bench, put his hands in his trouser pockets, stretched out his legs and surveyed himself.

Dodds and the German prisoner were hammering stakes into the ground preparatory to stretching wire across them for espaliers. Dodds said, "Hello, Master Rupert, nice to have you back again," and dropping the mallet he was wielding, started to pontificate about the war. The prisoner did not look up from unwinding the stiff wire from a fat coil. Rupert noticed that his slender fingers seemed unsuited to this sort of job.

"Now you needn't stop working just because I'm having a word with Master Rupert," Dodds directed, with a dismissive nod towards the German. The prisoner said nothing, continued uncoiling, from which indeed he had not for one instant paused, merely raised his eyebrows slightly and made a jutting movement of his jaw. Dodds, with hands on hips and a sweaty bowler hat pushed back from his forehead, availed himself of his privileged position to ventilate views on Sir Douglas Haig's tactics and Mr Lloyd George's shortcomings. At the conclusion of the dissertation he observed, with a jerk of the thumb towards the prisoner, "This 'ere ain't a bad bloke. Don't complain. Works moderate. Too posh reeley. Ought to be, but ain't, a n'officer. Comes 'ere on parole. I don't let 'im out of my sight of course, nor more than a minute. Will be sent for by a guard shortly; back to camp. 'Elps me, single-'anded, and don't do no harm neither. Most of 'em loiter around at our expense doing fret-saw and playing rounders."

"Schlachtball," said the prisoner.

"Don't interrupt me, my good man," Dodds said

6

with authority. "They leads an idle life on the whole, at h'our expense, the Jerries do," he continued, with surprisingly little rancour, considering that his only son had been killed twelve months ago, and resumed his monologue as though the German was not there. But as Rupert could see over Dodds's shoulder, he was there. The boy felt too shy to stare at Ernst, which he would have liked to do, at this enemy alien in his father's garden. He merely raised his eyes and catching the prisoner's eyes fixed for a moment upon his, lowered them, blushing. The disconcerting thing was that Rupert detected the suspicion of a smile of, he supposed, disdain flit across the German's face. It evaporated instantly. The German resumed the proud, slightly truculent air that had distinguished him hitherto. Presently he muttered, "Hier kommt der Feldwebel Leutnant."

"What are you saying?" Dodds asked. And addressing Rupert, "'E can speak English as good as me and you, when 'e wants to. And so 'e's going 'ome to 'is tea and cigars, 'e is."

A German non-commissioned officer and two elderly English corporals marched Ernst off to the prison camp. The camp occupied a neighbouring house in a small park which had been requisitioned for the purpose, and was presided over by a retired Lieutenant-Colonel from the Boer War. There were 123 prisoners of war under his control, nearly all German, with a sprinkling of Austrians, and two Turks whom the Teutons treated as outsiders. There were sixteen military officers looked after by twenty-five military servants, and thirty-six naval officers by as many naval servants. There were eight German cooks. It is true that the officers lived luxuriously. They had their own Amusements Committee, Wine

7

Committee and Cigar Committee. They were not obliged to work. The enterprising ones learned languages. Each officer had his own truckle bed and his own tin bath, but had to share latrines, all provided by His Britannic Majesty's Government. They had an adequate library on the premises. They got up plays and concerts. The men however slept on straw palliasses under four blankets, and had a bolster each. They indulged in carpentry, watch-repairing, boot-making, tailoring, football, hockey and "schlachtball". They were supervised by five Feldwebels, or praeposters, who were invariably unpopular with the men. Ernst, who was not an officer, did not choose to play games or work at a trade. Instead, after two years good conduct he had been granted permission to dig in Mrs Fiennes-Templeton's garden. The longer the war lasted the more lax the prison rules became. Those who were in daily touch with the Germans grew to realise they were not so very different from themselves; and the prisoners were too comfortable to risk the dangers and rigours of escape.

"Gute Nacht!" Ernst said without looking at Dodds or Rupert. "Morgen Ich wieder komme." He was hustled away by the guard.

(2)

"WE really must think of something useful for you to do," Mrs Fiennes-Templeton remarked next morning as she nibbled at a dried prune from a box which pre-dated the announcement of hostilities—the bread was so awful that she could not get it down without swallowing it whole, which induced alarming indigestion—"or you will wish you were back at school. And that would never do. If I don't rush now I shall be late, and Princess Arthur of Connaught is making her inspection this morning, which means . . . My goodness! It is 8 o'clock already." So once again she rushed off for the day, leaving Rupert to his own devices. Mercifully, she told herself, there was no mischief a boy of fifteen could get up to at Templeton, short of falling into the lake. And he could swim.

Nearly all the rooms in Templeton Manor were under dust-sheets; and downstairs the only one in use was the dining-room. The pictures on the mulberry brocatelle walls had not been moved. They were a mixture of yellowing landscapes—trees, a river, cows and a white horse—and portraits of men in armour, men in wigs, women with semi-exposed bosoms, and women with busts concealed up to the chin. But the large dining-room table had been dismantled, leaving the small round table in the window for eating. A few pieces of furniture had been introduced from elsewhere, such as the chintz sofa and two easy chairs, and Amy's writing-table which was strewn with unanswered letters and bills, awaiting Sunday morning attention after church. Rupert flung himself into one of the easy chairs, his right leg hooked over an arm. He took up Thomas Carlyle's magnum opus, his holiday task, and, beginning at the first paragraph, read:

President Hénault, remarking on royal surnames of Honour how difficult it often is to ascertain not only why, but even when, they were conferred, takes occasion in his sleek official way to make a philosophical reflection.

Rupert groaned, and turning the leaves to page 346 read, "End of volume 1." He got up and wandered into the garden. From the terraces he heard distant hammering. He would talk to Dodds. Instead of entering the kitchen garden by the iron gate Rupert shinned up the lean-to roof of the tool-shed, which was built against the high wall separating flowers from vegetables, and hoisted himself on to the coping. From this point of vantage he was able to look down upon the kitchen garden. Dodds was not there, and Ernst, in spite of the old gardener's assurance that he never let him out of his sight, was alone, at that moment squatting on his heels at the foot of a stake, with his back to Rupert. His ugly grey jacket lay on the ground beside him. He was in shirt sleeves, rolled above the elbow. Unseen, Rupert looked at him intently for the first time. He watched the muscles of a forearm ripple over the arduous labour. There, a few yards below him, was an enemy, a German, a devil, but a devil without a forked tail. At least there was no sign of one. Nor a pair of pointed bats-wing ears, which devils were traditionally depicted with. Instead Ernst's ears were small, close to the nape of a head poised upon a long, lissome back. These physical attributes contradicted Rupert's preconceived notions of what was fitting. Again he noticed Ernst's ridiculous hands, so unsuited to manual labour, as they fumbled ineffectually at wire and stake. The absurdity of it made him want to laugh.

Rupert began tapping the wall with his heels, at first gently. Flakes of loose brick fell like gentle rain-drops upon the lettuce leaves growing against the wall. Ernst, alerted, turned his head and rose to his feet. He scowled.

"How long have you been there, spying on me?" Rupert ceased tapping, but continued to stare without moving a muscle of his face.

"A cat may look at a king," he said. "An Englishman may certainly look at a Hun."

The prisoner flushed darkly. "If you were my son, I'd thrash you," he said. There was not a trace of Teutonic accent in his words. "I hate being stared at. and I won't stand it."

"Oh, but you'll have to," Rupert said. "What's more, I'll spit at you if I like," and he made as if to let himself down from the wall, which was at least ten feet above the ground on the kitchen garden side.

"Stop it, you little fool. You'll break your damned leg, and serve you right."

"Oh no, I won't," the boy said, and, instead of turning his front to the wall to lower himself by his arms from the coping, he stood up to jump feet first. Before he leapt Ernst sprang like a panther into the lettuce bed. He was just in time to break Rupert's fall. The full weight of the boy's body fell upon his arms. For a second or two Ernst, trying to remain upright, clutched Rupert like a sack of potatoes to his chest, before letting him slip gently to the ground. Rupert was conscious of the frenzied beating of the prisoner's heart against his own, and the warm flannelly smell of alien armpits.

At that moment Dodds appeared from his bothy at the far corner of the walled garden where he had illicitly gone for elevenses.

"Hi! Hi! on my lettuces. What h'ever be you doing? Get back to your job, Ernst. What the devil! The moment my back's turned too. And Master Rupert, good morning. Was he being h'impertinent to you?"

11

"Yes," Rupert replied, tucking his shirt back where it belonged behind the belt with a clasp like a serpent, "But of course I wouldn't let him."

Ernst turned to Dodds and in an impassive and dignified manner said: "Mr Dodds, the young gentleman, in spite of my warning, insisted on jumping from that wall. I caught him just in time to prevent an accident. That is the truth of the matter." Then he went back to his work as though there had been no interruption.

Zigzagging from one side of the road to the other Rupert pedalled laboriously up a steep hill. At the top he dismounted and let his bicycle fall sideways on the grass verge. The front wheel, twisted upwards, spun round with a petulant whirring sound like a swarm of bees. Rupert lay on the ground beside it. He was bewildered by the course his thoughts had taken. Had they run away with themselves? Could a man mistake for his own thoughts those of another? Lying on his back with his face towards the immaculate blue sky Rupert re-enacted in slow motion the morning's experience. Not knowing why he had decided to jump he merely allowed his memory to record the seconds while he stood on the top of the wall before taking the plunge. The German had acted as though by precognition. Rupert again saw the look of anxiety with a trace of anger on his face as he dashed to the foot of the wall. He recalled too pressing his toes against the coping and lifting himself into the air. Without any guidance he fell against Ernst's chest. He felt Ernst quiver with the impact but sustain it. He felt a slight pain in his crutch as it landed against the man's firm thigh. Then he recaptured the absolute relaxation, the surrender,

12

and almost before these sensations could be registered, the slide down his legs to the lettuce bed. What he could never forget was Ernst's eyes, mere inches from his own. The sloping brows, the deep-set sockets, the ruthless yellow light, as of an eagle's, encircling the orbs. The whole business lasted seconds, not minutes. In an agony of shame Rupert rolled over on to his front. The nobbly earth bit into his knees and thighs. With outstretched hands he grasped at tufts of coarse grass as though they were hairs.

He jumped to his feet, picked up the bicycle whose front wheel was now slowly rotating, remounted and sped downhill. The glorious, earned reward of the freewheel, bringing that indescribable release from all inhibition, was his. Arrived at the bottom Rupert pedalled easily along the flat. A thrush darted from the humped surface of the road into the blackthorn hedge. Languorous clumps of dog's mercury and young un-blooming cow parsley bowed in the wake of his speed.

(3)

"RING the bell, dear. No, I don't mean that. Run and ask Pritchard to clear the tea things, will you." Mrs Fiennes-Templeton for a moment forgot the war. She did this sometimes when she was very tired. She was wonderfully convinced that when the war was over life would return to normal. It never entered her head that it might be different.

"I have to sort through this ghastly knitting," she said, indicating a pile of comforters, scarves, socks

13

and Balaclava helmets which the ladies of the village had worked during the past week for their men in the trenches. "You might like to help me." Rupert who could hardly claim the calls of a more urgent commission reluctantly consented. He held at arm's length each object which in turn his mother, screwing up her eyes, examined stitch by stitch, before putting neatly into piles. Rupert admired the dexterity of her thin fingers and her deft precision. Those garments she regarded as below standard were thrown aside and a note was pencilled in a worn schoolroom exercise book against the name of whichever lady must be exhorted to do better next time. Pritchard, who had been bustling about at the far end of the room, patting cushions, folding the newspaper and flicking dried mud disposed by Rupert's outdoor boots on the sofa, was tut-tutting. "Some young men know how to make work for others," she complained.

"Now, really Rupert, you don't have to lie on the sofa all day with your dirty boots on," his mother joined in. "Your trouble is that you've got nothing to do."

"Except scare the wits out of some people," Pritchard interjected.

"Whatever do you mean, Pritchard?" Amy enquired.

"Mr Dodds will tell you, m'm. He nearly had a heart attack this morning. And Master Rupert's no light weight to be sure when it comes to his felling you to the ground from mid-air."

"What are you talking about?" Amy put on a martyred look in anticipation of some disagreeable communication calling for her intervention.

"He jumped off a tree straight on to him, that's what he did. Mr Dodds said he's never had such a fright in his

14

born days. And his heart none too good neither."

"Rupert, I'm ashamed of you. It isn't as though we had the full complement of gardeners these days without your risking the life of the only one left us."

"I'm sorry, Mother, I really didn't mean to." He was thinking how odd it was that either Pritchard had got the story all wrong, or old Dodds lied to her because he should not have left the German prisoner alone by slinking off to the bothy for a glass of cider.

"You really *must* find something to do besides playing the fool," Amy harped on the same old theme as though the finding lay quite outside her province. "You cannot lounge around all day and every day." She did not expect a response. She received one.

"I have decided, Mother," Rupert spoke out. "I would like to work in the garden with Dodds. For the rest of the holidays. May I?"

Amy was certainly not one, during a time of shortage of staff, to look a gift horse in the mouth, even her own son. Nevertheless she was surprised, and suspicious. Pritchard merely raised her eyebrows.

"Give him sixpence an hour, m'm," she suggested.

"Sixpence!" Amy almost shouted. "I think three-pence would be overdoing it. But I will consent to fourpence."

Rupert stuck to the compromise. He did not begin his labours so early in the morning as Dodds and Ernst because his mother insisted that Rupert's hours of work must not overlap her spare hours from the hospital. Sunday gave little enough time to spend with her son without surrendering his society during those hasty weekday breakfasts when she was in a hurry and high teas when she was usually too exhausted to be companionable. She was conscientious enough to wish to keep an eye on him. She wanted to get to

15

know him better. He was such a reticent boy. Rupert accepted her measured advances, not with relish, not with positive revulsion, but with polite regression. She felt like a person with bad breath close to another who recoils.

"Well, you must do whatever Dodds tells you, dear. But don't mix with the German more than necessary. And don't let him boss you about in any way whatever. I must rush now," Amy said on the following Monday morning at 8 o'clock.

When Rupert reported to Dodds for duty in the kitchen garden the old man was bedding annuals. He did not regard his absent master's instructions to neglect the flower borders as extending to prohibition of cultivating a few pansies among the cabbages for picking purposes, or even those grapes and nectarines in the greenhouse which had survived the lack of central heating. Dodds, having been primed by Mrs Fiennes-Templeton, gave Rupert orders just as if he were a newly engaged garden boy. Ernst who at Rupert's approach was on his knees a few yards away neither looked up nor uttered a word of greeting. All that day and the next and the next he maintained a studied silence, merely nodding obediently whenever Dodds issued him instructions. Rupert might not be present for all the recognition he got from the German. Duly at 1 o'clock Rupert withdrew to the house for his luncheon, returning punctually at half past two. At five he was allowed off. For several days Dodds did not absent himself at eleven o'clock and the two subordinates were not left together. Towards the end of the week Ernst took a long ladder which he propped against the sycamore tree with a view to sawing off a dead branch. Rupert in an initial gesture of friendliness approached the bottom of the ladder to steady it.

Already half way up the rungs Ernst looked down, waved the saw at the boy dismissively and growled, "Nein! Keep off!" Rupert was offended.

One morning Dodds, who previously had brought his elevenses in a paper bag to eat on the steps of the potting-shed, slunk off to the bothy for a glass of cider and a pipe. Rupert and Ernst were for the first time left alone together. Rupert put down his tools and with hands on hips turned to the other and said gently, "I am sorry, Ernst." The acknowledgment he got for this *détente* was the single word, hissed through the German's teeth – "Shit!"

"Shit?" Rupert echoed interrogatively. "What's that?" Ernst in his turn dropped his tools, placed his hands on his hips and gave the boy a prolonged look of intolerable disdain. He did not vouchsafe another word. It was their sole communication in the first week.

(4)

MRS Fiennes-Templeton was apt to be late for high tea on Friday evenings. Pritchard was arranging the silver tea-pot between the silver milk jug, of which the bottom was barely covered by a substitute made of powder and water, and the silver sugar-basin which contained three lumps. She stepped back to admire her handiwork by casting her head to one side. The blue ribbons from her cap fell upon her right shoulder. Rupert said, "Pritchard, what does *shit* mean?"

"What does what mean, dear?" she replied.

"I said *Shit*."

"Never 'eard of it, but it sounds a rude word to me."

"I think it means a fool."

"Well, perhaps it does. I wouldn't be too sure," she said.

Presently Amy came in, threw off her V.A.D. hat, sat down at the table and began pouring from the tea-pot. A colourless liquid trickled from the spout.

"Why, Pritchard! You've forgotten to put the leaves in the pot," she said, slightly nettled.

"Gracious me, m'm, so I have," Pritchard exclaimed, astonished.

Rupert piped up, "Oh, Pritchard, you *are* a shit."

"What funny words you sometimes use," Amy said disinterestedly. "Where do you get them from?"

"School, I suppose," Rupert said, keeping his head. It was evident to him that his mother knew no more German than Pritchard.

A fortnight went by. Rupert worked conscientiously. Dodds reported very favourably to Mrs Fiennes-Templeton who was gratified and amazed. But what kept Rupert at the job was the proximity of Ernst. In spite of the German's overt hostility he sensed an intangible bond being woven between them. In his taciturn companion he felt harnessed to a mysterious dynamo which impelled him to labour almost as unremittingly as Ernst himself. He was undeterred by the indifference towards him of the young prisoner who, whether himself aware of it or not, had become his motivation and control, like the sun keeping the earth within orbit and totally dependent upon its gravitational pull. One afternoon when Dodds had walked into the greenhouse out of earshot Rupert, who was hoeing not two yards from the German, again took courage and whispered, "Sorry,

18

Ernst." At this Ernst stopped, focussed his hawk's eyes on Rupert's small, freckled face, pierced him to his very soul and, as though involuntarily, allowed his thin lips to part in a cold smile. Then he hoed the trench vigorously in the opposite direction.

The last week of the Easter holidays had begun. On Monday morning Dodds went for a longer break than usual to the bothy. Rupert decided he had nothing to gain by the unbroken silence. He had learned through one of nature's instinctive processes that a man gets nowhere without taking initiative. It was a grey, drizzling day. He and the German were in the potting-shed on either side of a trug basket full of bulbs. They were sorting them. Inadvertently Rupert took hold of a bulb which Ernst's hand had reached first.

"Sorry, Ernst," he said gently for the third time, and was about to withdraw his hand. In a flash Ernst seized it in his, and holding it with a grip of iron said, "Yes, Ruprecht, I accept your apology because you are too young to realise when you have insulted a man of honour. If you were older I would not be taking your hand, I would be hitting that little girl's face of yours. Yes, Ruprecht, Ich bin Deutsch. I am also a gentleman. You should realise that."

Rupert could have shouted with the pain of the handgrip. He went white.

"I see I am hurting you as you hurt me when you fell on to my chest that day," he laughed, actually laughed, showing small, white, regular teeth. There was an unexpected fullness about his mouth which Rupert had not noticed before. The nostrils of his straight nose flared like those of a hound long confined to kennels which suddenly snuffs the scent of a fox cub.

"I have been wanting you to be my friend," Rupert said. "You may not think so, but I am almost as lonely

19

as you must be—I have never had a friend. Will you forgive and be my friend, Ernst?" There was a pause before Ernst replied.

"You've an odd way of looking for friendship. But yes. I'll forgive you. I shall be your friend—your brother." He leant across the trug, put his hands on Rupert's two shoulders, steadied him and, moving his head closer, kissed him on the lips. "There," Ernst said, withdrawing his dark head and moving his hands to cup Rupert's face a foot from his own, "There," he repeated, "that'll be our pledge, won't it? We shall keep it to ourselves, shall we not? We won't tell anybody else."

Still holding Rupert's head in his earth-encrusted hands Ernst assumed so unwontedly gentle, almost humble an expression that the boy felt tears tingle the backs of his eyes. Either because he was afraid to cry, or because the turn of events left him absolutely spellbound, Rupert just managed to force the one word, "Yes," before he rose and bolted from the potting-shed.

In the kitchen garden he met Dodds returning from the bothy.

"Anything the matter, Master Rupert?" the old man enquired not unkindly.

"No. Yes. I have an awful tummy ache, Dodds," he managed to say, belatedly clutching his stomach. He continued running and on reaching the iron gate turned round. The gardener was watching him.

Rupert could not go to the house. Although his mother was out Pritchard would be there, asking teasing questions why he had left work so early. Instead he wandered into the pleasure ground towards the lake, hardly knowing where he was going. He was elated and shocked. His mind was in such a daze that he could not, had anyone questioned him, explain either what had happened or how he felt. Had he been blown sky-high by a German howitzer and escaped death by inches he would not have been more agitated or bemused. He meandered idly along the margin of the lake, casually picking up pebbles and throwing them into the water. The mallard indignantly gathered wing and scuttled across to the island. The drizzle turned to light rain. He made for shelter in the Temple of Flora, one of those sedate classical follies with a facade adorned by a Roman pediment supported by a pair of columns. A tall doorway led to a chill and dank interior. At the far end an alcove enclosed a damaged bust, presumably of the goddess, on a pedestal. Against the side walls a pair of wide benches in the Chinese Chippendale style faced one another. The seats were covered with thick fitted mattresses, stuffed with some hard straw-like substance, the faded covers, once worked by industrious fingers, now sadly deteriorating through damp and moth. Rupert pushed open the heavy door, which grated against the paved floor, entered, and sat down.

What had he done? What had happened to him? On calm reflection what did he feel? Disgust? Guilt? Remorse? None of these things. Why should he? Perhaps he ought to be ashamed? He wasn't. If she knew, his mother would be scandalised. Rupert began to revel in a fantasy of the tortures he would undergo sooner than disclose to a soul the new friendship made and sealed so solemnly. Their mutual act of pledging, in the exchange of each other's breath, the touch of tongues, the commingling, not of blood but saliva, and the taste of the other's very being, aroused such rapture that Rupert felt rather frightened. Henceforth customary mundane habits, brushing one's teeth,

21

customary duties, making conversation with grown-ups, customary pleasures, eating sweets or bicycling, would merely become perfunctory performances in an unreal world. What would be real was the new plane into which the true "he" would for ever exist, secluded and protected. Such are the innocent pipe dreams of the young and insecure. He felt that he had achieved victory.

When Dodds walked into the potting-shed Ernst was squatting on his heels busily sorting bulbs, un-shaken, austere, cold, subserviently polite. "What's happened to the lad?" Dodds asked, apprehensive on his own account for having left the prisoner of war alone with his employer's young son.

"I don't rightly know. I think he was taken ill," Ernst answered in a voice of utter impassivity. "He just left. I have finished this job, Mr Dodds. What do you wish me to do next?" It was evident to the gardener that there had been no trouble between the two. He was relieved.

When Rupert, having missed lunch, returned to the house Pritchard said, "Why, your shirt is soaked through. Have they let you work in the rain then, the silly shits?"

"No, I had a stomach ache," Rupert said, "and I walked in the park to get rid of it." He was by now outwardly composed.

"That was a funny thing to do," she said. "You'd better run upstairs and change before your Mummy sees you."

(5)

WHEN Mrs Fiennes-Templeton came in that evening she was more tired than usual. Rupert on the other hand was in a state of ill-concealed euphoria. His eyes transmitted an unnaturally bright light and he walked about the dining-room as though treading on air. To his mother's complaints about the gruelling work she had undergone that afternoon he responded with uncustomary solicitude. He exhorted her to put her feet upon the sofa, removing her shoes with his own hands lest, as he pointed out, she might leave mud on the chintz cover, and hurling them into the air like a juggler. When one of them got stuck on the brass electrolier he gave vent to uncontrollable guffaws of laughter.

"I can't see that there's much to laugh about," his mother said, "with the news as bad as it could possibly be. You realise that if the U-boat sinkings continue this country will soon be reduced to starvation. Besides, there's your poor father involved at this very moment fighting for his life in the Champagne."

Even mention of his father's dilemma could not extinguish the flame of happiness burning in Rupert's heart. Nevertheless he became solemn.

"I think it must be because the Americans have come in. We are bound to win now," he said.

"But they haven't prevented things going from bad to worse, that I can see," was Amy's gloomy reaction. "Those damned Huns giving no quarter. Torpedoing merchantmen and allowing, positively allowing, every man on board to drown. Discarding the immemorial courtesies of the sea," she waxed rhetorical in her indignation and quoted from a leader in the newspaper. "The devils!"

23

"Mother, are you sure that all Germans must be devils?" Rupert asked, wide-eyed. "Don't you think a few, two, or even one might be different from the rest? Should we hate the whole lot? After all there must be millions of them."

"Yes, the whole damned lot," Amy replied, rather flushed. "If I had the power I would wipe the entire nation off the face of the earth. And don't let me ever hear a son of mine say a good word for a single one of them."

"No, Mother."

After this explosion Rupert knew how precariously he walked. He would keep his own counsel. If his mother felt like this then his father, who was at close quarters with Germans, must presumably feel the same way. Every patriotic Englishman must. Since he no longer did, he was a traitor, and if he was a traitor it would not matter what other bad thing he might become in addition. Although he did not use the expression, he might pile Pelion on Ossa with, if not impunity, then without multiple damnation.

Next morning Rupert returned to work in the garden as usual. Dodds greeted him with a kindly, "Feeling better, Master Rupert?" "Yes, I'm fine," the boy answered.

"A temporary h'indisposition then," said Dodds portentously.

Ernst, who was a few yards away digging, did not look up, far less commiserate or enquire. Not a muscle of his face twitched. "Hard-hearted bastard. They're all the same," Dodds muttered to himself. He did not retire to the bothy that morning, but ate his sandwiches with Ernst, the two of them chewing in silence. The whole day long Rupert was unable to have a word with Ernst; nor received from him so much as a glance.

On Wednesday Dodds retired to the bothy, and the English boy and the German man were again left together. Rupert put a hand on Ernst's sleeve.

"Ernst," he said sadly, "I am going back to school first thing on Saturday morning."

"Oh." And a shadow passed across his face, "then you won't be a gardener boy any more in the daytime?"

"No. I shall be away for three whole months."

"Three whole months. That is a long time. It is a boarding school then, is it not? I forgot you English boys are sent away from home. How barbarous. I shall not see you at all."

"No. But we shall remain best friends, shan't we? We made a pledge, didn't we? You won't change, will you?"

"I shall remain your friend, kleiner Ruprecht, if that is what you mean," he said enigmatically.

"It is what I mean," Rupert said. He gave the other a look so trusting that only a beast—and Ernst was not that—could deliberately ignore it. Instead Ernst continued:

"We have to consummate our friendship, haven't we?" He spoke with that same tenderness which had kindled in Rupert a vibration from the bottom of his spine to his brain when the pledge was made in the potting-shed. Ernst's wild eyes seemed to liquify. "Yes," the boy replied hesitantly, for in truth he hadn't a notion what the other meant and was too shy to admit it.

"Wasn't the pledge a promise—for ever?" His voice expressed anguish.

"Yes, we promised to be very special friends for ever. But a promise is a promise. It isn't a fulfilment. We don't even know what each other is really like."

25

His eyes were scanning Rupert's body. He was smiling now. "It is essential that we know each other deep, deep down. Why, we haven't even talked together!" He was changing key for he sensed the other was out of his depth. "You don't know what I am, nor I you." He was grave again. "We must be quite alone together, not here in this wretched kitchen garden with old Mr Dodds. We must have a clandestine meeting, as you call it. We must arrange it before you leave. By night perhaps when nobody is about, where we can be by ourselves. Just think of that—if only I can get away."

"Oh, do manage to get away," Rupert insisted. "Do you think you can? There is only tonight, or tomorrow, or Friday."

"It is not as easy as you may imagine," Ernst said. "We prisoners are closely guarded. And you realise I would be shot if they caught me. But on Friday the officers have staged a concert in the camp before the Commandant. Most of the warders will be attending. I do not play, my services will not be required. I have friends. I will slip out at 8.30 when it is nearly dark. It takes me twenty minutes through the wood. I can meet you at 8.50 prompt." He was working the scheme out carefully in his head, screwing up his eyes in the process. "Where can we meet?"

"Do you know the Temple of Flora, by the lake?" Rupert asked excitedly.

"The classical temple close to the large tulip tree. I have once been inside. It is the only one?"

"It is the only one. I can be there at ten minutes to nine, without fail."

"But you are sure you can get away without being seen, kleiner Ruprecht? You will have finished your dinner by so early an hour? It is the hour when one dines, surely."

Rupert laughed. "No longer. My mother and I have high tea at 6 o'clock. Then we play cards for half an hour. Then we both go to bed."

"Sehr bürgerlich und gemütlich. Ja."

At that moment Dodds's dirty white panama hat—for the sun was again at its late April trick of feigning summer and dictating the gardener's wardrobe—could be seen bobbing above the privet hedge from the bothy.

"Oh Ernst, if anything should go wrong I will leave a note for you in the little hollow at the back of the bust in the Temple. Or I could always find one from you there. But it won't go wrong. 8.50, Friday then."

"8.50, Friday."

They separated and when Dodds came round the corner they were attentively and silently at separate tasks.

(6)

RUPERT had much to consider. The prospect of being quite alone with Ernst, without fear of interruption, of being able to enjoy his presence for as long as he wanted, to talk to him freely, to question him about so many things, to "know" him, as Ernst had expressed it, without old Dodds's shadow hovering over them, and the location, beside the lake in the slightly sinister Temple, after dark too, were as alluring as any adventure contrived by Baroness Orczy for the Scarlet Pimpernel. Rupert identified himself with the indolent, mysterious British aristocrat, Sir Percy Blakeney, who rescued victims from the guillotine. Did Carlyle mention Sir Percy in his boring book? He doubted it. Rupert's role was to offer temporary succour and comfort to a prisoner of war on the run. It was practically the same thing. He did not see himself as a victim.

On Thursday evening Mrs Fiennes-Templeton came downstairs to high tea later than usual. Rupert was eagerly sniffing the nettle soup, the scrambled powdered eggs and the acorn coffee kept tepid on the steel plate-warmer, beneath which the single methylated spirit lamp bravely maintained a thin blue flame. Pritchard was as usual fussing with knives and forks.

"It is quite extraordinary," Amy said, looking from left to right as though expecting to find what she had been desperately searching for staring her straight in the face. "Your father's little gold pencil. I could swear it was in its usual place on the writing-table in his dressing-room before I came downstairs this morning. I wanted to jot down a note just now; went to pick it up. Not there. I've searched everywhere. Not a sign of it. It's most mysterious. No one has been in the house today, have they, Pritchard? I mean no plumber, or electrician? No one from outside?"

"No one, M'm, that I'm aware of, and I've been here all day. It isn't often I goes out these days," Pritchard responded huffily.

"What a very funny thing," Rupert said, while he raised himself in his chair to watch a large blackbird with yellow bill chase a similar blackbird on the lawn outside, while a dun, complacent hen, the wife of one of the males, stood unconcernedly in the background. "A very funny thing," he repeated absent-mindedly.

Amy was genuinely distressed by the loss of her husband's cherished pencil which his father had given him on his twenty-first birthday. It had his cypher incised in blue and white enamel, and was indeed no ordinary pencil, having been bought at Fabergé's shop in St Petersburg. Besides, as Rupert knew, she regarded it in a proprietory way and liked to use it as though it were as much hers as his father's. This he always resented. Nevertheless when the exiguous meal was over—Rupert's hunger was seldom assuaged—she played a hand or two at coon-can with her son. The habit was what she called relaxing her nerves. Rupert's concentration was not on the game. He was rehearsing in his mind tomorrow evening's escapade. Yes, at half-past seven his mother started to yawn, seeming bored by her son's company. But it did not do to retire before eight o'clock, not that she went straight to sleep then. She went to bed, and read, and this was when silence reigned throughout the large empty house; Rupert would have to take the utmost care not to disturb it.

Sure enough at five minutes past eight Amy gathered together her things on the sofa, her book and reading spectacles, rose, kissed her son on his forehead, said good-night and went upstairs. Rupert ambled across the paved hall. After standing at the front door to survey the nightfall, the quiet descent of twilight and the almost boisterous revival of loud bird song before roosting, he looked towards the lake and the temple out of sight behind the great tulip tree. Then he exercised his privilege, as deputy master of the house, of turning the fat key in the massive brass lock. This done he turned towards the staircase and, as noiselessly as possible, mounted the shallow treads barefoot. On tiptoe he passed his mother's bedroom door. He reached his own several doors further down the first-floor passage.

The following morning before leaving in her usual hurry after breakfast Amy said, "Oh, I quite forgot, dear, to tell you last night—it must have been worry about the pencil—that this evening we are invited to have a bite of food with the Tulkinghorns. We so seldom go out and it is your last evening. I am sure it will be fine. We can go on our bikes. I think it will be rather fun. I shall be back earlier than usual from the hospital."

Rupert, who was carrying a cupful of acorn coffee, which he had just poured for himself at the side-board, to his place at the round table, nearly swooned. He recovered himself and sat down. The news was so disconcerting that he was struck dumb. He could not at first utter, and he felt faint. This Amy noticed.

"You don't say anything. You don't like my little plan? What a difficult boy you are to please. You know you are fond of the old Tulkinghorns, and their granddaughter, what's her name, may be staying with them. Aren't you feeling well?"

"Yes, perfectly," he managed to stammer, which turned out to be a fortunate tactic, although the consequence of no deliberate strategy. "I am sure it'll be fun." The words were ground out like a handful of corn from old mill wheels. His mouth was so dry that he could barely articulate the words.

The situation was desperate. With only one solution. He must be ill; yet not so ill that his mother or Pritchard would feel obliged to sit up with him at night; yet not so little ill that his mother would go out to supper by herself, thus on her return coming to his room on her way to her own. He must of course be too ill to go out himself, yet towards the evening so much better that he could plead a desire to go to bed early, and sleep undisturbed. This is what he cunningly contrived.

To deceive Pritchard in the middle of the morning (during his mother's absence) into believing that he had a temperature was easy enough—a glass of hot water hidden under the bed into which the thermometer would be plunged while her back was turned. Towards the evening his temperature would be normal and he brighter, possibly bright enough to have tea with his mother before retiring early to his bedroom. The wheeze worked.

He did not go to the kitchen garden this last morning of the holidays. After his mother left the house he told Pritchard that he thought he might have got 'flu.

"Now if that ain't a nice coincidence the day before returning to school I don't know what is," Pritchard exclaimed. "In that case, off to bed you go, young man. If you ain't well enough to work in the garden you ain't well enough to hang around the house." And she packed him upstairs. "And when you're nicely tucked up I'll come and take your temperature." This was duly done, and Rupert had time to run the bathroom hot tap long enough to fill a tooth tumbler and conceal it under the valance.

Pritchard was enjoying herself. She shook the thermometer so furiously that Rupert feared the mercury end might fly off. She plunged it into his mouth. "And don't you bite it," she warned. "I once knew a little girl what had to have her stomach cut open and the broken bit extracted." Rupert began a gurgle of remonstrance which was checked by Pritchard resuming: "And don't talk neither. If you do, it won't work, apart from the dangers aforesaid," she added. "I'll be back in five minutes."

This allowed Rupert ample time to give the thermometer a good soaking in the tumbler. On hearing

Pritchard's returning footsteps he thrust the burning end back into his mouth.

"Mercy on us!" Pritchard exclaimed, desperately turning the glass implement round in her fingers at the window lest she had misread the figure. Her eyes were none too good in spite of the thick lenses of her gold-rimmed pince-nez.

"What is it, Pritchard?" Rupert enquired nervously. Had he overdone it?

"You'll stay in bed all right, young man. And at 1 o'clock I'll bring yer a cupful o' Benger's." That was not at all what Rupert deemed sufficient, but for love, he thought, one must be prepared to endure material privations.

In small communities news spreads quickly. In less than an hour Dodds was saying to Ernst in the kitchen garden, "Master Rupert won't be coming this morning. 'As a 'igh tem-per-a-ture. Seems 'e 'as the h'influenza bad."

Clearly Pritchard's wise precautions and the Benger's Food had averted the onslaught of serious illness. By the early afternoon Rupert's temperature was normal; by five o'clock it was positively sub-normal. When Mrs Fiennes-Templeton got home soon afterwards she was informed of developments. She was not altogether surprised for she had noticed how pale he looked at breakfast. Did she not always discern when her boy was out of sorts? So it was not the sulks which had struck her as his only conceivable objection to supping with the Tulkinghorns that evening. Of course he could not now bicycle there. And she could not very well go without him. A pity, when she had made a special effort to entertain him. But she knew her duty. She would stay with him. She would put a call through to the Tulkinghorns and explain.

32

Rupert was not allowed to get up for tea. Instead his mother had a fire lit in his bedroom to which Pritchard carried a tray. Mother and son together ate a modest meal. Rupert was ravenous and had to restrain his appetite. He also had to restrain the rattle in his stomach by squeezing it hard whenever he heard the threatening cannonade.

"Well!" said Pritchard as she came into the bedroom panting in anticipation (like the White Queen in *Through the Looking Glass*) of stacking and lifting the heavy silver tray of used plates and cups, "I've never known such a rapid recovery, not in all my born days, I haven't." Amy was more sympathetic. She stayed talking to Rupert for half an hour, asking about his prospects of getting into a higher class next term, asking him what he wanted to do when he left school, speaking of his father's gallantry and love of them both—and even touching upon the delicate subject of honour. She had the utmost faith in Rupert. He would never, she was confident, do anything to bring dishonour on the family name. He knew what she meant, she felt sure, without having to particularise. It was odd the way that gold pencil had disappeared. No doubt it would turn up somewhere. It must have been mislaid in the dusting. She could not press the point further with Pritchard who was so touchy. Meanwhile she would give her boy a couple of aspirins, tuck him up for the night and leave him to sleep soundly. She would not disturb him again. And she went down the passage to fetch two dry white pills and a glass of water. Rupert's effort to swallow several sips of the water while tucking the pills between teeth and cheek, make the appropriate grimaces, smile, thank and allow Amy to kiss him on the perfidious cheek itself, called for concentration, skill and aplomb.

By the time his mother left him it was not yet dark, although she had drawn the curtains before closing the door. For several minutes Rupert lay supine, his head propped on pillows, motionless, with his thoughts. They were racing round his head. His pulse was pounding with anticipation of the unknown, and dread. When it subsided the first thing he did was to eat voraciously a large slice of seed cake which he had managed to slip off the tray while his mother's back was turned. This helped assuage the worst pangs of hunger. Then he looked at the round tin clock, crowned with a large bell, which ticked loudly on the bedside table. The hands pointed to 7.35. There was not all that much time before he would have to leave. He continued to lie and listen. What an age his mother was taking to undress! Ah, he heard her bedroom door open and her soft footsteps approach down the carpeted passage. She was going to the W.C. That done, she retreated to the accompaniment of clanking and hissing of the cistern, back to her bedroom. She was collecting sponge and towel. He heard her footsteps fade in the opposite direction towards the bathroom. Amy's bathing was a rapid operation. In the first place she disapproved of soaking in the bath. It was an ennervating, not to say, decadent habit. In the second place, by this stage of the war she had had a thin red line painted round the bath-tub a bare three inches from the bottom in accordance with that patriotic gesture instigated by His Majesty the King. Even if the most ancient and immobile squires and their ladies could not forward the war effort in any other way, by this sacrifice they could salve their consciences and share, albeit vicariously, to some extent the discomforts of our boys in the trenches. Almost before Rupert finished reflecting

34

upon these matters his keen ears heard the tiny ration of water his mother allowed herself gurgling through the plughole—all the plugholes at Templeton gurgled—before hissing down the waste pipe to join the rainwater pipe where the magnolia grew against the east wall of the house. Within a few minutes he heard the sharp click of the brass bolt of the bathroom door draw back while his mother, swathed in her inelegant Jaeger dressing-gown and trailing a faint scent of "Quelques Fleurs" bath powder retreated to her bedroom. Within five minutes she would be immersed in Sir Oliver Lodge's *Raymond or Life and Death* by the light of the brass bedside lamp with ruched pink silk shade. For an hour, or even two, she would read.

Rupert's clock did not strike the hours, which was just as well for the noise would have been deafening to judge by the cacophony made by the alarm bell at 7.30 each morning. Instead when the large hand reached the hour the bell emitted a strangulated click. Rupert waited till it reached ten minutes past eight. Then he got out of bed. He dared not switch on the electric light. He drew back the curtains. The twilight filtered reluctantly into his bedroom, which was streaked with shadows.

Rupert took off his pyjama top and put on his thick winter vest with half-length sleeves. In his haste he left undone the three chest buttons, one of which was anyway missing. He put on a white cricket shirt with open collar and sleeves stopping short of the elbows. Kicking off pyjama trousers he donned woollen pants which did not quite cover the knees; then tweed breeches, pepper and salt, necessitating the agony of buttoning them below the knee by means of a button-hook. The process involved pinching the bare skin while drawing the buttons through

35

their respective holes. Then a pair of striped braces to uphold the breeches by means of six loops from as many buttons. Then, a pair of knitted stockings to reach the breeches, and a pair of woollen garters wound round the tops which were turned down. The garter ends hung loose in two little bobbles over the calf of the leg. Lastly, the tweed waistcoat, and over it the Norfolk jacket, reefed at the back and belted. He was ready. Ah yes, he remembered the present. He reached for the clock, whose ticking now seemed to declaim his errand of wickedness. He opened the back and extracted from the movement a small envelope which he thrust into the inner pocket of his coat. And now for the descent without betraying himself. He carried his boots under his arms.

He shut the door very gently behind him, releasing the handle so that the latch fell into place smoothly, and stood for a second in the passage. How could he explain himself if his mother were to appear at her door? There was not a sound beyond the slow, measured ticking of the grandfather clock halfway down the front stairs. Then far away, a floor board creaked. But it was not his doing. He paused. His mother's light shone like a streak of gold beneath her door. He crept in his stockings towards the baize door which led to the back stairs. Pritchard by now would be in the servants' hall, where she sat up late with Mrs Staples, the cook, their feet on the brass fender, knitting, far away out of sight and sound.

Having descended the back stairs and advanced to the hall Rupert made for the front door. Upon a tall hat-stand, festooned with his father's numerous felt hats, straw hats, and even a dusty billy-cock, hung his own multi-coloured cricket-cap. He jammed it on the back of his head at a nonchalant angle, a tousled forelock of hair falling below the up-turned peak on to his forehead. Perching on a hall chair he put on his boots, criss-crossing the laces over six pairs of hooks. The leather lace of the left boot broke under the strain. Never mind. He opened the front door with ease. As he did so the grandfather clock boomed the half hour.

Rupert knew by heart every square yard of the garden and park. Besides, night had not yet fallen. It was that magical moment, *entre chien et loup*, when earth and sky were as much lit by a waning moon, scurrying through clouds just over the tree-tops, as by the dying rays of sunset. The two elements were poised between silver and gold. The wind of day had subsided. The sparrows had ceased chirping. All nature was suspended. The earth was spinning into the silent universe. Rupert made his way along the grass strip beneath his mother's windows before tiptoeing over the crunching gravel drive which separated house from terraces. He walked down the terraces and looking back saw a crack of perpendicular light between his mother's bedroom curtains.

His feet swished through the long grasses, already drenched in evening dew. Soon he was at the margin of the lake. Not a moorhen stirred. Just a plop in the still water as a languid roach rose for the last lunge at a midge. The tulip tree loomed very high and menacing. And round the corner appeared the portico of the temple.

Why on earth was it dedicated to Flora, Rupert wondered, thinking of the beautiful goddess of fruits and flowers who, married to Zephyrus, the west wind, was crowned with blossoms in her hair and enjoyed perpetual youth? She would not have resided in this gloomy, sinister temple, not for an instant. He was unaware that some early Romans had regarded

37

her as a whore who acquired enormous riches by prostitution and every sort of lasciviousness, in celebration of which these cynical people instituted a yearly festival out of respect for her earnings. He walked up the three steps. In the dusk he noticed that the heavy door was half open. His heart beat with an unknown fear until he remembered that he must have left it ajar when he went there the morning he took the pledge with Ernst. It seemed years, not days ago. Then he was still a child. Now he was an adult of sorts. At any rate there was no drawing back. Quietly he slipped through the opening. It was dark inside, and for some seconds he could distinguish nothing.

How unwelcoming the temple was. He sat on the hard mattress of one of the Georgian benches which was partly hidden by the half open door. It must, he calculated, be at least a quarter to nine. He waited. Perhaps after all Ernst was not coming. Perhaps he never meant to, and had merely been fooling him. Perhaps he had been unable to leave the camp. Rupert thought of the cavity behind the bust. He went up to it and put a hand into the hollow place. He touched the bottom. His fingers felt dust. There was no note inside. He took from his coat pocket the small packet and dropped it into the cavity. He would tell Ernst to look for it there. It would be a pleasant surprise for him after he, Rupert, had gone back to school. He turned round. Again he waited. Suddenly the room grew noticeably darker. He could see nothing through the door opening. It was in shadow. The shadow shifted. He detected a faint glimmer of the sky's reflection in the lake. His heart stood still. He gripped the pedestal of the bust to steady himself. But he did not stir. He heard a faint rustle and saw a narrow beam of light search the interior, pass over the plaster ceiling, from which damp patches of moss and gelatinous cobwebs were suspended, search the paved floor, the wide Chippendale bench on the left, then that on the right, then the arch of the alcove, before dropping upon the noseless head of Flora. Instantly his frightened eyes were struggling against the round gold glare of a torch.

"Ruprecht!" The torch fell to the floor with a clatter, the light went out, and the shadow became a shadow again. It enveloped the whole interior of the Temple, and, moving like an eclipse of the sun across the earth's surface to where Rupert was crouching, enveloped Rupert too.

"Oh, Ernst!" he said, "I thought you wouldn't come."

"You thought I wouldn't come. I thought you couldn't. How is the influenza? Was it very bad? And how quickly it is over."

"That's what Pritchard said."

"Oh, I guessed it when old Dodds said you had a very high temperature."

He understood. He knew. Their arms entwined. Together they stumbled unsteadily in that manner in which only a pair of earthbound lovers with four legs between them, or gods depicted against the laws of gravity on the clouds of ceilings, can stumble, and fell upon one of the Chippendale benches.

"How cold you are, kleiner Ruprecht. Your hands are frozen. Let me warm them. And I will give you a temperature again." Ernst hugged him.

They did not speak. Rupert thought, "This is the essence of knowing." Presently he said:

"Why do you speak English almost like an Englishman? Not even like a good foreigner, except when you speak it too well."

39

"There. You insult me again. Always you will insult me," Ernst replied. "I will explain. It is so easy. My mother is English. My nurse and my governess were English. I went to a school in England. My father died when I was small and, although I am German"—his chest swelled—"I am also half English. Now you see. And then came this war and because my Kaiser told us to fight you English, I had to. I was not in the army more than six months when I was captivated. And here I have been for nearly three years your neighbour, your servant and now your slave. And you insult me as though I were a dog. That is what there is to it."

Rupert raised his head. He began to laugh. "You were captivated in battle. Now you are captured by me." And he dissolved in merriment. Ernst felt the young body shake within the circumference of his arms. So close were their faces that his was flecked by a fine spray from the boy's lips. In a flash he was angered. He stifled the mocking laughter with a violent kiss, the force of which all but choked Rupert that he thought he might die of it.

"Oh!" Rupert gasped when his mouth was released. "Oh God!" This was terrifying. His lips, his tongue were on fire. His chin stung as by a swarm of bees. He struggled to be released. He felt, though he could not see, so close they were in the darkness, those hawk's eyes boring a hole into his skull. He felt the spark of their yellow light from the sunken, slanting sockets burn whatever of him it touched. It was like that pin-head of sun through a magnifying-glass when at school they set alight dead leaves. He was a dead leaf. At school it was forbidden. It might set the class-rooms on fire, they said. He would be set on fire.

"Ernst!" he cried, but his voice sounded as a

voice sounds when muttered through a wall. "Now I understand. Now we have consumed each other."

"We have what?"

"Consumed each other. That's what you said we'd do."

"'Consumed', my feet!"

"Foot," Rupert in his turn corrected.

He relaxed his grip on the boy's body, which went limp. Rupert felt like a rag doll that has been dropped into the gutter, paralysed, not in command of his movements, no longer himself. Ernst said he was a babe in arms. On the contrary he was a prisoner. He experienced what it was like to be deprived of will, with protest to no avail. The awful truth was that a man could become putty merely under the scrutiny of another. Total submission was the only consequence, and defeat excused the most degrading humiliations.

Gently Ernst laid him full length on the bench. He took off his own grey jacket and folded it under Rupert's head. He knelt beside him on the hard floor.

"And you live in a big castle?" Rupert asked irrelevantly.

"Damn you, I possess some big castles," Ernst answered impatiently. "My mother is looking after my biggest castle for me. But we do not speak of castles now." What was the boy thinking of? Was he totally bereft of a sense of occasion? The German suddenly and immutably relented. Innocence was not the fruit on which Ernst habitually fed.

"Yes, little Rupert," he said, "and when the war is over, you will come and stay with me in the holidays. I will look after you."

"Will you really? Do you promise that I can live with you for ever and ever?"

"Why, of course." He demurred. "But of course."

"I don't yet know where your home is. I don't even know who you are."

"I will write my name and address for you on a piece of paper. I cannot do it now. I will put it in the place behind the bust with a broken nose and you will find it when you next come home."

"Oh, Ernst, how wonderful. Promise faithfully to do that. The broken nose. I think you have broken mine too, and the whole of me." He raised himself and threw his arms round the German's neck. He buried his face between his friend's chin and shoulder, clinging to him, while the other's strong arms supported his back. He felt the long fingers idly scamper over his back. He felt Ernst's right hand gently stroke his open throat. He smelt the warm breath on his cheek, felt the dry lips brush the lobe of his ear, heard the subdued but insistent murmurs of interrogation. Were they words? What did they imply?

"Ernst, are you here?" he asked, seized now with misgiving.

"Of course I am here. What do you mean?" Ernst knew full well what was meant.

"Oh, I just wondered. Part of you is here. But the other half seems to have gone away."

"The half that matters is here, little Rupert."

"I see. Only one half of you, whichever that is," he answered, and made a sound between a laugh and a sob.

"Whichever that is," said Ernst beneath his breath. In the Temple of Flora, under the sightless gaze of her mutilated bust the young man and the boy lay together, unmoving, in oblivious silence.

42

Rupert's sharp ears caught a sound beyond their mingled breathing. He strained them. Could it be? His name being called? Not once, but twice, and a third time. "Master Rupert!"

"Glory!" he gasped. "Quick!" He slithered from the German's arms to the floor. Shook himself like a dog from water, picked up his rumpled coat and cap, and darted out of the temple door. He ran as fast as his legs would carry him. Then slackened his pace. "Master Rupert!" Pritchard's voice called again, closer. She too was waving a torch just below the second terrace.

"Here I am," he screamed, the tears choking the words. "I'm coming!"

(7)

ERNST had also heard the third cry into the night. Alerted by the sudden tension of Rupert's body he had gripped the boy with all his might, digging his nails into the small of his back; but Rupert's response to the calls was so instantaneous and his surprise so fearful that Ernst relaxed his hold. Before Ernst had time to consider the meaning of the situation Rupert, with a dexterity that made Ernst marvel, slipped from him like an elver from a dense tangle of weed down the rapid current of a stream. And was lost to him.

Ernst sat on the end of the bench with his head in his hands. So that was that. He was so taken aback that for several minutes he could not believe he was once again alone. Over these barren years he had grown a carapace of apparent cynicism. Now the quarry had

43

been snatched from him and bitterly Ernst, forgetting all pride, gave vent to a torrent of tears. They trickled through the cracks of his tight fingers and flowed in a rivulet to his elbows.

He pulled himself together, stood up, felt for his ugly grey jacket which so short a time ago he had folded and placed under Rupert's head, shook it and put it round his shoulders. He felt for the torch on the floor. It was broken. When he stepped out of the temple there was enough light from the waning moon to guide him through the wood whence he had come alone less than an hour previously and through which he was marched to and from the Templeton garden every weekday by a small posse of guards. Individually the guards might vary from day to day, but a fairly regular member was a sandy-haired, middle-aged English corporal, known to him and the other prisoners merely as Sam. This man was his friend in so far as he had a friend in the camp. Certainly Sam was a tacit ally. It was he whom Ernst had persuaded to smuggle him back into the camp this evening. Sam was a simple fellow with a kind heart. Too old to be drafted into a fighting regiment and too little educated to be of use in the Intelligence Corps he had been recruited from the village to serve under the Camp Commandant. To him the war meant nothing beyond a change in his circumstances from milk roundsman to corporal. To the German Kaiser's territorial ambitions, the invasion of Belgium, the reported atrocities of Uhlans and U-boats he was as indifferent as a duck's back to water. Sam did not share the intense hatred of the majority of his fellow countrymen for the Germans. Having worked at least two years among them he saw little difference between them and his own people. They ate their food with a

44

knife and fork, did not mess up the latrines, in fact were rather tidier and cleaner than the average English labourer, sang similar songs, laughed at similar jokes, chased balls on the playing field, and smiled nicely at him. Of course they spoke an outlandish language, but they could hardly be blamed for that. Somehow Ernst was exceptional. He spoke English. He was clearly better educated than the rest of the prisoners. Besides, though haughty with his German colleagues, Ernst always addressed Sam with an artless politeness. Sam felt sorry for the handsome young German who was hardly more than a boy himself. He took pity on him. He was soon bringing him chocolates and cigarettes from the village shop, even writing-paper, pens and ink and other luxuries not supplied by the camp stores. For these commissions Ernst never failed to reward him handsomely. Whereas the other men were niggardly with their pocket money Ernst seemed quite unconcerned and was prepared to hand over whatever sum was required without turning a hair.

Beyond these legitimate transactions Ernst had never yet trangressed. He had never asked for any favour which might compromise Sam's authority or bring upon him criticism from the Commandant. Sam regarded him as a law-abiding prisoner who had long ago abandoned the prisoner of war's traditional obligation to attempt escape, if indeed he had ever seriously contemplated it. So when Ernst approached him with the unusual request to turn a blind eye when he walked out of the camp tonight during the concert, and let him in again about two hours later, Sam consented. The smile from that remarkably handsome face, normally so sad and grave, accompanied by an almost affectionate pat on the shoulder and the diffident offer of a fiver, merely as a present and not

45

a bribe for services, to accept which would be doing the donor a favour, Sam found irresistible. He may have thought that Ernst, being a poetic sort of chap, merely wished to seek inspiration from the solitude of the wood by night, and if he did have—which Sam supposed unlikely—an assignation with a woman, who could possibly blame a lusty young fellow of twenty-three denied all physical outlet month after month?

When Ernst emerged from the wood which separated the Templeton park from that of the house now converted into the camp he saw the long windows of the hall in which the concert was still taking place ablaze with light. As he got closer he heard the excruciating clang of an upright piano striving to outdo the screech of a pair of fiddles and a 'cello in an appalling rendering of Grieg's piano concerto. Ernst was not a performer but he was a passionate lover of music, having attended concerts and opera in Berlin and Dresden. It was an agony for him to catch even a few bars of a concerto which he knew well being mangled by a group of amateurs who would have been just as contented mutilating a popular music hall song. He walked round the high barbed-wire fence enclosing the camp to the make-shift guard-house. This was the only entry. He was too early. If Sam were on duty he would not be expecting him yet. He paced up and down the wire fence, trying to block his ears to the gruesome strains of the tortured Grieg issuing from the open windows. At last, after a short encore, the performance was over. The few friends and relations of the Commandant would be leaving. Ernst hovered cautiously round the guard-house. He heard the heavy oak which sported the great door drawn back. Sure enough there appeared the crumpled, un-military figure of Sam, his puttees collapsing in a spiral heap over his boots, silhouetted against the naked white blaze from a paraffin lamp. He beckoned to Ernst to approach; then raised an arm in warning to stay where he was. There was a clamour of voices and scramble of nailed boots on a concrete floor. Then an urgent summons. Sam without ceremony grabbed Ernst by his belt, literally pulling him inside the door with the strength of a mechanical hoist lifting a sack of potatoes on to a truck. The Commandant, a sergeant and two other corporals were talking with animated gestures to a couple of civilians about to depart. The group was too preoccupied to notice Ernst's entry. Nevertheless Sam with a wink spoke sharply to Ernst, asking him what the devil he meant by being in the guard-house and ordering him to return to the hall instantly and help stack away the chairs and move the piano to its customary place under the staircase. Ernst was safe. All he need fear now was enquiries from his mates as to what he had been doing all evening.

In his bunk his thoughts turned to Rupert. How had the poor little boy explained to the dragon of a parlour-maid and presumably to his mother why, after being in bed all day with influenza, he had dressed surreptitiously and gone for a walk by himself in the dark? Having endured that ordeal Rupert would now be lying on his bed in a state of unhappiness Ernst hardly dared to contemplate. With the knowledge that nothing had changed for the better and that there was no reason for supposing the war would not drag out its weary length for years to come, he ultimately fell asleep.

(8)

"WELL, he just managed to catch the train in time," Mrs Fiennes-Templeton explained to Pritchard who was handing her a glutinous macaroni cheese for Saturday luncheon. "But only just. I had to persuade the station-master to stop it while the engine had already got up steam. The driver backed it of course so as to allow me to shove Master Rupert into the luggage-van where the platform slopes down to the line. It was that dreadful old tin lizzie of Jenkins's which had a puncture on the way to the station and, can you believe it, another puncture on the way back."

Pritchard could well believe it.

"I feel completely worn out. What with the anxiety lest we missed the train and the bad mood Master Rupert was in."

"Mr Jenkins says he can't get them spare parts what is necessary for a proper taxi fit for the quality," Pritchard observed. She was inclined to be on the defensive of her own class, whenever criticised. Besides, Jenkins, like nearly everybody else in Templeton village, was her second or third cousin.

"I was speaking of Master Rupert's extraordinary mood," Amy went on. "I cannot think what is the matter with the boy. Usually he is very unhappy when he is returning to school. In fact I sometimes have to be quite stern with him in case he cries. But this morning there were no tears, no regrets. He merely seemed broken, utterly broken as though the cares of the world were weighing upon him; and so silent. He hardly uttered. And when he did, said he didn't mind if he were alive or dead. He said goodbye to me as though

I were a casual acquaintance whom he did not mind if he never met again. As to his behaviour of last night I am mystified, Pritchard, totally mystified. Have you any explanation?"

"No, madam, I haven't. That I haven't." Pritchard was speaking the truth.

The previous evening Pritchard was knitting in her chair with her feet on the fender and chatting to Mrs Staples the cook, seated in her chair in front of the empty grate of the servants' hall. In the Templeton household Mrs Staples was a shadowy figure in all but bulk, which was very considerable. Harmless, well disposed, slow-moving and negative she was the perfect foil to Pritchard who so dominated her that she had long ago abandoned a pretence of having a mind of her own. She was moreover so frightened of her mistress that whenever Amy entered the back regions of the house she fled, if such a verb is appropriate to one of her comparative immobility, to the water-closet where she locked herself in. Amy considered her half-witted, which she wasn't entirely, never gave her orders direct, but always issued them to her through Pritchard who rejoiced in their delivery and interpretation. At least Mrs Staples was a companion to Pritchard for the two women were the only servants left in the large, rambling back regions with their seemingly endless stone corridors, store-rooms, still-rooms, unused laundries and makeshift lean-tos.

Pritchard knew her mistress's ways. She knew that once ensconced in bed by 8.30 nothing, short of a zeppelin raid—an unlikely contingency in darkest Staffordshire—would rouse her from it; certainly not the well-being of her son. Pritchard on the other hand, being devoted in her own way to Rupert, felt moved to see for herself whether he was all right and

49

asleep. Abandoning her knitting and rubbing the thick lenses of her spectacles with the fringe of her apron she announced to Mrs Staples that she would creep into Master Rupert's room just to see how he seemed. She did so. She opened his door gently and hearing not a sound of breathing called his name in a whisper. There was no stir of the bed-clothes. The curtains of the window being drawn back a faint light from the moon etched a creased black outline of the sash bars across the sheets of the bed. Although she had just polished her pince-nez Pritchard was unable to detect the familiar outline of Rupert's sleek head on the pillow. She drew closer and felt the bed-clothes which were turned down in a jumble of untidiness. At first she thought the boy, having heard her approach, was playing a trick and perhaps hiding under the bed. She retreated to the door and switched on the light. The opaque white saucer shade suspended from the ceiling shed a cruel glare upon white emptiness.

"Now then, Master Rupert," she exclaimed, worried. She looked under the bed and inside the wardrobe. She looked at the chair on which he had thrown his day clothes. They were no longer there. Instead his pyjamas had been flung as though hastily over the back. Pritchard returned to the servants' hall, imparted what she had discovered, or rather not discovered, to Mrs Staples, who without raising a succession of double chins from her protuberant bosom, or pausing in her crochet, merely exclaimed, "I never."

"I am going to look for him," Pritchard said, "but I won't tell the missus until necessary." Whereupon she put on her blue serge cloak, seized the master's torch which reposed on the hall table next to the letter-box, and left the house by the front door. It being unlikely that Rupert had gone off on his bicycle which Pritchard knew had no front or rear lights, she descended the terraces, where, as we have already heard, she began calling him.

"And did he give no explanation at all why he was out in the park at dead of night?" Amy resumed, while she chewed disconsolately at the macaroni cheese. Pritchard was still hovering over her.

"None at all, m'm. He wouldn't say nothink, beyond . . ."

"Beyond what, Pritchard?"

"Beyond his having a fancy to go for a walk in the moonlight."

"But it was a crazy thing to do after being in bed with a high temperature. What can have been the real motive? It isn't as though he's interested in birds, and wanted to listen to a nightingale. There is something very odd about that boy. I don't know, I'm sure. I don't seem to get through to him. He no longer takes me into his confidence. I suppose he was ill yesterday. How high was his temperature when you took it in the morning?"

"110, m'm."

"A hundred and ten!" Amy ejaculated. "But that's impossible. He would be dead by now in that case."

"I assure you, m'm," Pritchard bridled, for she did not relish her statements being questioned, "the mercury had quite reached the end of the glass tube. Scalding hot it was too. Almost burnt me fingers touching it."

"But you say it was normal by five o'clock?"

"By five o'clock it were sub-normal, under 98 degrees," Pritchard said, drawing herself up.

"In other words he did not want to go to the Tulkinghorns for some unknown reason, and faked a high temperature," Amy deduced, as a police detective at Scotland Yard might deduce after weighing the pros and cons of an extremely complicated criminal action. "He didn't want to go to the Tulkinghorns. And why not? That is now the question. In order to go for a walk in the pleasure ground in the dark. Dear me, if only the Captain were here (since the outbreak Amy liked to refer to Joshua by this title rather than the usual one of Squire; it sounded slightly more democratic, since we were all in the same boat those days; at the end of the "duration" she would revert to the customary nomenclature). "It is all too much for me, what with this place, my work, and now a recalcitrant son. If you do hear anything, or come upon a clue to his behaviour, you will let me know, won't you, Pritchard?" she asked pathetically.

Pritchard was not so sure that she would. But she kept this reservation to herself.

"He said twice, if he said it once," Pritchard chose to remember, "whiles I put 'im back to bed, and before you heard us talking and came into 'is bedroom, he said, 'Oh, I do wish the war would end. I do wish the war would end.' Quite piteous he were."

"Ah, that may explain. He worries about his father at the front. He wants him safe back. That's what it is. Poor boy. You know, Pritchard, I think he is a little too old for his years."

"Yes, they does grow up too sudden by far. Before you can say Jack Robinson they gets ideas," was the parlour-maid's enigmatic reply. She had been sorting the weekly linen from the laundry basket that morning.

"They suddenly understand the sadness of situations. It's no bad thing when they come to worry about the absent parent they love. It shows a good

52

disposition. He has always admired his father. Perhaps it is because he has seen so little of him. Whereas I am here all the time. He takes me for granted in consequence. But I don't blame him for that."

"Yes, they worries about the person they loves," Pritchard murmured as she turned to leave with the silver tray.

"And now," said Amy, "I must go through his things in his bedroom, tidy up the dreadful muddle he always leaves, and throw out some of the rubbish he has collected in the holidays." She did not add that she would have a good search in his drawers for the lost gold pencil.

(9)

CORPORAL Samuel Pritchard usually had Sunday afternoons off. Before going home to his cottage and wife and children in the village he would stroll across to the manor to have a gossip and mug of strong tea with his sister and Mrs Staples. Olive, for that was Pritchard's christian name, had far more news to communicate than Sam's mousey wife. Besides, she was more fun. As for Mrs Staples she liked Sam and listened with a fixed smile above her chins and a fusillade of twinkles from her minute brown button-eyes to his weekly account of the goings-on in the camp. Sometimes she would nod her head with approval, but beyond this heavy gesture she seldom ventured an opinion.

"And how be things?" Sam opened proceedings in the servants' hall where there was no fire because it was war-time, although the room which had high windows that could not be looked out of and seemed as though sunk below the level of the earth, was dank and chill. He warmed his hands round the large earthenware mug filled to the brim with black tea and a sprinkling of powdered milk.

"Just as usual. It isn't us what has the news as a rule," Pritchard observed. Mrs Staples gave the slightest indication of a confirmatory nod. "Master Rupert went back to school yesterday."

" 'E be gettin' a fine young fellar these days?" Sam remarked, vaguely questioning.

"He don't seem to be growing very fast, leastways outwardsly," his sister answered.

"Well, there be plenty o' time for that," said Sam after a deal of reflection. "Has Mrs Staples a nice bite o' cake for a poor, hard-working soldier, I wonder?"

Mrs Staples had in a tin on the dresser a slice of cake which, without owning to it, she rose with much struggling from her chair to fetch.

"And how are things at the camp?" Pritchard asked in her turn.

"Oh, not too bad. There be changes coming, I'm informed. Some prisoners will go, and some will come. They be dead set on not keeping 'em too long in one place. They fears mischief, it seems, without swopping around. They doesn't want us to get too friendly with the Jerries. And after months it is hard not to feel sorry for some on 'em. Not but what they are all nice, mind you."

"You prefer some to others?" his sister enquired.

"I do. It's natural, ain't it? Some are downright up-stage, some are h'indifferent, and some are so friendly-like you would take 'em for Englishers."

54

"Yes, I understand that."

There was a pause in the conversation while Sam sipped with loud sucking noises from the mug until his sister resumed, "And do you see much of the young fellow what comes to work in the missus's garden? Now there's a nice looking lad, though I says it as shouldn't, for all he be a Bosch."

"Indeed," answered Sam succinctly. The British guard at the camp were strictly enjoined not to discuss the prisoners with neighbours and Sam prided himself on his discretion.

"Mr Dodds tells me you often marches him from the camp to the kitchen garden, and fetches him of an evening."

"Yes, I does that." Sam was non-committal.

"And he told me, Mr Dodds did, as how there were a grand concert got up by the prisoners last Friday. I guess young Ernest be a dab at an instrument. Would it be the pianer, or the fiddle 'e plays? The fiddle, I guess."

"No, it ain't neither."

"You don't mean to tell me that a young man like that ain't a musician, he so well spoken with the English and so educated, Mr Dodds tells me. Well, I am surprised."

"There's much in life to be surprised at, Olive," Sam said with profound insight.

"Indeed there is for sure. And we've had something happen our end to surprise us right enough."

"What be that?"

"Oh, nothink that would interest you, I daresay."

"Something wrong with the missus?" Sam's alert hearing did not escape his sister's notice.

"No, no, she be all right. Same as usual, neither better nor worse. But Master Rupert, he's been all

55

upset lately. Working himself into a state all about nothing as we can see. Threatening to do himself in and walking about the park the better part of the night."

"No, you don't say. When be that then?"

"On Friday last," she said, "before going back to school yesterday morning. But it wasn't nothing to do with school for he didn't mind whether he went back or stayed here, which is the first time I've known him not mind the end of the holidays. Mark you, 'e's a good boy and wouldn't get up to no mischief, I'll be bound."

(10)

AMY Fiennes-Templeton was a woman deserving of some pity, although she received little from those who knew her. Her two brothers had been killed in the war and her elderly father had subsequently died. Few could remember her mother and she was seldom referred to, as though she had somehow brought discredit upon the family. Amy was envied for her inheritance, and for being the wife of Joshua, a casual, good-natured extrovert with no pretensions but with the skills appropriate to his station as a landowner. And Amy was the mother of a healthy boy who, if there were laws of good breeding, ought to be her pride and joy. But she appeared as a woman drained of sympathy, aloof, straight-laced and humourless, although she filled her role as lady of the manor with precision and politeness. Her acquaintances attributed this off-hand manner to her bereavements, which were common to practically every adult alive in the Kaiser's war, but they failed to sense—how little do we see inside the hearts of our neighbours, how seldom do we spare the time to investigate – that she was longing for companionship and love.

The lot of a good-looking woman—though slightly too much on the tall side—aged thirty-five, isolated in a large, cumbersome country house with a commensurate estate, for the management of which she had received no training, working voluntarily five and sometimes six days a week as a hospital sister, for which likewise she was ill-equipped, remote from London, its theatres, suppers and dancing, was hard indeed. Joshua seldom got leave from France and when he did their reunions were not exactly jubilant. She was not so insensitive as to be unaware that, while partnering her on the polished boards of the Savoy grill-room he was looking over her shoulder at little balls of fluff or anticipating adulterous delights of the morrow. These oblique glances were gall and wormwood to her self-respect and her heart.

In Amy's fairly short life the past three years had been less enviable than those of her more adventuresome female contemporaries who went overseas, drove Generals in large touring cars to the front lines, or even served in canteens in South Kensington. Her stay-at-home jobs at Templeton and in a small provincial hospital were, although she did not recognise it, souring her.

Having turned out every cupboard and drawer in Rupert's bedroom, taken stock of his holiday clothes, emptied pockets, put aside those garments he had outgrown and those which needed mending, having filled a large waste-paper basket with a miscellaneous assortment of objects, bladeless knife-handles, bits of string, a tube of secotine, broken pieces of a Meccano set, old tins and even *Tiger Tim* annuals—the boy was too old for such rubbish—Amy turned to other humdrum duties which received little attention during the week. There were the wages to be paid and the store-cupboard to be replenished. There were also the tiles on the harness-room roof to be repaired, the scullery tap to be given a new washer by whatever builder and plumber could be bribed to attend to these trivial but essential tasks. There was Dodds to be talked to. He came every Saturday afternoon, hat in hand, to the back door. Pritchard having directed him to wait in the gun-room would inform the mistress that he was present. Dodds always needed new tools, seeds, or manure, things about which she knew little and cared less. He reported on the vegetables he had planted and the poor results caused by one or other of those pestilential predators which haunt the lives of gardeners. He carefully omitted to refer to the flowers and fruit he secretly cultivated and reported on the conduct of the German prisoner whom she had never had the curiosity to see. This time Dodds asked permission to take a day off, whenever convenient, to go to the dentist. It was a nuisance but could not be denied. When this boring interview had taken place, there were the accounts. Amy dreaded the accounts more than any other occupation. She had never been good at mathematics and subtraction was quite beyond her. She spent hours wrestling with the infernal figures, biting the end of her pen-holder until the paint came off on her lips. Bills and letters would be left over till Sunday morning after church. She never failed to write once a week to Joshua and, when he was at school, to Rupert.

Thus events dragged on at Templeton. May came and almost went without a break in the dreary regime.

Joshua wrote that he was shortly to be transferred to the Near East but he feared without the prospect of any intermittent leave. He could give her no idea when they would next meet. Rupert's letters were wholly uncommunicative, deficient in any apparent interest in what was happening at school and without curiosity about life at home. Worse still, his headmaster wrote to Mrs Fiennes-Templeton complaining that the boy showed no pride in his work or, what was more inexcusable, his games, was off-hand with the assistant masters, positively rude to the matron, and seemed indifferent to to his erstwhile school chums. At first Dr Halliday had charitably attributed this lackadaisical attitude to ill health. But on the school doctor assuring him that nothing was the least wrong with Rupert physically he could only suppose some mental strain was oppressing him. Boys approaching adolescence sometimes experienced similar symptoms to those of the menopause in women, and if this was what Rupert was suffering from then he, Dr Halliday, had never come upon a worse case. Could his mother inform him if he had been subjected to some grave emotional disturbance during the Easter holidays. He could hardly suppose he had over-worked at Carlyle and Cicero since his papers on these tasks had been the worst of all the boys in his class, and showed little sign that he had even read the two classics allotted. He even hinted that, unless Rupert pulled himself together before the end of term he might be obliged to ask for his removal, or at least temporary suspension from school until he recovered his manners and *esprit de corps*.

This was a difficult letter for Amy to answer. She was bound to admit to Dr Halliday that during the last few days of the holidays her boy had been rather moody. She interpreted his behaviour as concern over the course of the war and anxiety about his father who, as the headmaster knew, was in the thick of the fighting. She begged him to be lenient and assured him that she would write her son a severe reprimand which was bound to have the desired effect. In fact the very idea of Rupert being superannuated, or sacked as she preferred to express it, filled her with terrible alarm. The dishonour would be ineradicable, and people would almost certainly misinterpret the reason for something much graver and more unmentionable than mere passive insubordination. She and his poor father would have no option but to send the lad to the colonies with a fiver in his pocket, never to be heard of again. In any event it would be a dreadful bore having him at home hanging around her, even for a matter of months.

(11)

ONE fine afternoon Amy found herself alone at Templeton. Pritchard and Mrs Staples had by long pre-arrangement and with their mistress's consent gone off on a day's jaunt with other women in the village to Birmingham. They had left at 5.30 in the morning by wagonette to the nearest railway halt where a special train was to take them the rest of their journey. They would not be back until 11 o'clock in the evening. The expedition had been looked forward to with such excitement that the phlegmatic Mrs Staples had had diarrhoea for three days beforehand, and it was very much feared might

60

not be in a condition to join the party. But by dint of a diet of some extremely binding nature she managed to throw off the disorder just in time. Amy who had agreed that it was suitable the two women should enjoy a treat for once, although there was a war on, volunteered, with the permission of the hospital matron, to stay at home during their absence in order to take care of the house.

The weather had lately been beyond compare, as is often the case in the middle of May when it portends ceaseless wet throughout the rest of the summer. Although the magnolia on the west front of the house was no longer in flower the chestnut candles were in full bloom. The elm, sycamore and beech trees had reached that pinnacle of lush green which another twenty-four hours without rain would reduce to a faded ochre. The unmown, unscythed grass of the terraces was languid with umbelliferae, starry white woodruff, golden buttercups and some slender purple columbines which had strayed unbidden from a neglected flower border. A very faint breeze wafted the sweet scent of may blossom from the hedge which years ago had been planted in order to obscure the untidy back regions from the view of callers approaching the house up the drive. Amy stood enjoying these natural delights until—for she was no botanist or gardener—they palled. She retreated to the dining-room, now the only living room, to read, leaving one of the tall sash windows of the big bow open at the bottom. But she was restless and ill at ease, being unaccustomed to absence from the hospital on a weekday. Somehow it did not seem right to be idling. She could not concentrate on her book. Her eyes wandered round the room. They lit upon Rupert's gramophone, a small square box-like

61

instrument with circular turn-table and an absurd brass horn attached to the sound-box.

Beside the gramophone lay a linen-covered album containing records, so slotted into sleeves that the title of each record was disclosed through a circular opening below the familiar device of a white terrier cocking an ear to catch the sound of His Master's Voice. Amy flipped through the heavy pages. A waltz of Johann Strauss would be nice. "But no, I must not play music composed by a *Hun*," she said to herself out loud. A song from the *Merry Widow* would be just the thing, but that too was ruled out for having been composed by an Austrian. Amy finally selected excerpts from *Remembrance* and *Dreaming*, delicious tunes in the Victorian music-hall tradition of her youth, and composed by an Englishman. Like so many withdrawn and rebarbative people she was inclined to secret nostalgia. She also craved romance. She would like to be swept off her feet by, well—a sheik. An absurd confession, she knew, and shameful too. Mrs Fiennes-Templeton of Templeton Manor. Nevertheless she wound the handle which protruded awkwardly from the back of the sound-box like the steering apparatus of a tram-car. Protesting groans and squeaks issued from the bowels of the instrument. She selected from a small tin a new needle—how often had she not warned Rupert that old needles ruined records—dropped it into place on the upturned stylus box, switched on the mechanism and gingerly lowered the needle upon the outermost groove of the black revolving disk. At first an amplified hissing issued from the horn, followed by an agonised note several times repeated in a sort of choking hiccough. Needless to say Rupert's clumsiness had caused a crack on the record. Deftly Amy picked up the stylus and lowered the needle on to an inner groove. Instantly without any preliminary bars the reverberant notes of a waltz rang out loud and clear. Now it happened that whenever Rupert turned on the gramophone Amy was irritated. Alone, with no fear of being overheard by her son or the servants, she could concentrate on the melody. Indeed she revelled in it.

Amy recalled the occasion when she had danced to this music with Joshua. It was not a success. He had complained that her feet were too large. She had been hurt and mortified. It was not as though he were an expert dancer himself. Far from it. She caught her reflection in the long pier-glass between the windows in the wall adjoining the bow. Being a very old glass with bevelled edges the mercury had perished in places so that the surface was mottled with a mauve shadowy film. Nevertheless the glass reached down to the floor skirting so that she was able to make a thorough examination of her feet. She turned them out this way and that. Admittedly she was tall, but no well-disposed person could justly complain that her feet were out of proportion to the rest of her figure, which was slim, even svelte. Somewhat archly she put her hands on her hips, slid them down her thighs, stretched out her bust and drew in her stomach, thus accentuating the narrowness of her waist. Then she turned her body sideways and her head to face the looking-glass. Her bosoms were still marvellously taut and full, their outline in profile, she considered, faultless. Her back was straight as a ramrod and her neck, which Sickert had once walked across a room to praise, high and finely shaped. It did not sit on her body like a T-square turned upside down, but sloped gracefully to her shoulders in that way which she admired in Turner's ladies at Petworth, and which no doubt Sickert had admired too. Before she could appraise her head and face the gramophone ground to a ghastly sepulchral halt. The damned thing needed re-winding.

Amy attacked the handle ruthlessly as though she bore it a grudge, and rather roughly turned back the arm from which the needle was suspended so as to play the same waltz over again. Before return. . o the pier-glass her attention was drawn to a decante. on the side-board. It was one quarter-full of port wine which nobody had touched since Joshua was last on leave. She herself never drank more than an occasional sip of Sauternes at a dinner party, and not even that in wartime. She remembered King George V's prohibition of whisky, a horrible concoction by which she had never been tempted. Deciding that port was not at all the same thing, she would try some. What a devil she was being, on a weekday too in midsummer! She poured herself out a glass and took a large gulp. She resumed the survey of her reflection.

With the rhythm of the waltz she allowed her head to nod in a coquettish manner, at the same time assessing with particular satisfaction the shape of her nose and mouth. There was nothing the least wrong with the contours of either, except severity. The nostrils were tight; the lower lip was turned down at the corners. These were not faults of nature, but indications of her prevailing sorrows. They could be rectified. She stood there, gently swaying, endeavouring to flare the nostrils and turn the contours of her mouth upwards. Yes, that was more conciliatory, if not positively inviting. What with her grey-blue

64

eyes and chestnut hair scooped back loosely in a neat bun and the regularity of her features she could, if only there were someone to appreciate her, assume a gentle, even seductive appearance, although she admitted to herself that a houri's manner was not natural to her. It could be assumed only for a fleeting moment. She could no more keep it up permanently than a deaf person could keep a trumpet in his ear day and night on the chance visit of a stranger who had something to say worth hearing.

Amy took another gulp of the delicious, sweet, tawny syrup. She re-wound the gramophone and for the third time played the same waltz. She felt inordinately relaxed. Back to the looking-glass, hands again on hips she swayed languorously to the music, this way and that. She bowed, she bobbed, she jiggled, she twirled, she pirouetted. Round and round she went, now clasping her hands to her bosom, now holding them at arm's length, now throwing her head back, now thrusting it forward, now clockwise, now widdershins, always in front of the glass, and never losing sight of her reflection. She was waltzing with fervour, skill and elegance, by herself. The music stopped. Crack, crack and again crack, went the needle as it passed over the final groove, back into the penultimate. Out of breath, elated, she stopped, ran across to the gramophone and with the flick of a finger switched it off. It growled, and died.

Amy sank exhausted on to the sofa. Spreading her arms along the back of the sofa she stretched her long legs across the carpet, half reclining. The skirt of her frock had worked its way above the calves of her legs. In this indelicate posture she raised her eyes. Good God! A man was standing, his back to the strong sunlight, in the open bow window. He was motionless. He was facing her. For all she knew he might have been there half an hour. When she recovered from fright she became angry. Her eyes suddenly lost their brightness; her nostrils resumed their tightness, her mouth turned down at the ends. Amy became Mrs Fiennes-Templeton with a vengeance. Gathering her legs together and tugging at her skirt, she sat bolt upright.

"Who are you, pray?" she asked imperiously.

The figure advanced out of the glare of the window into the shadowed room, and stopped respectfully a few paces from her.

"What is the meaning of this? Your behaviour? It's most unorthodox. I do not know who you are, taking this liberty. Please explain yourself." Pritchard and Mrs Staples had often said, or rather Pritchard had said while Mrs Staples nodded assent, that the mistress would scare away any burglar merely by looking at him.

The intruder spoke. "Madam, I am very sorry if I am taking a liberty. And sorrier still if I have caused you an uneasiness."

The voice was instantly recognised by Amy as being what she customarily called cultivated. It was that of a gentleman, albeit there was something a trifle foreign about the intonation and pedantic about the delivery.

"Since Mr Dodds is away today, madam, at the dentist's, and omitted to give me instructions what to do when I finished weeding the paths, I thought it would be in order for me to approach you direct. I could get no response from the back door bell and so, on coming away and hearing music, madam, I knocked on the open window."

Ernst was not strictly telling the truth. Dodds was indeed away at the dentist's and his long delayed appointment had conveniently coincided with the women's outing to Birmingham. He had gone with them in the wagonette. Ernst saw no harm in conveying to the mistress that the old gardener had not forewarned either her or the camp guard of his impending absence, and that the latter evidently so trusted him as to leave him unattended. It was a fact that the guard—Sam was on this day not one of them—were by now thoroughly bored with the daily delivery and retrieval of the prisoner and being confident of Ernst's trustworthiness had not bothered to look for Dodds in order to hand him over. But Ernst was pretending that he needed instructions. He happened to be aware that Mrs Fiennes-Templeton was alone, was curious to have a look at her and see how much she resembled her son. At once he noticed how slight the resemblance was in appearance and personality.

Amy continued to stare at him amazed. "And your name is?" she asked. "Ernst, madam," he replied. His manner and mien were so correct that Amy was taken aback. She rose to her feet—it is always wise during an embarrassing encounter to be on one's feet—and walked to the fireplace. There, leaning one elbow on the mantelpiece she felt more secure. Besides, the light was off her face and now on his. What she saw was a very young man, quite astonishingly handsome.

"Then you are the German prisoner who works in my kitchen garden?"

"Yes, madam." He was standing at attention. The serious face had no expression on it whatsoever. It might have been that of a wax effigy in Madame Tussaud's. Amy was disconcerted. A touch of insolence would be preferable to this daunting impassivity. She took in the upright figure from which the ungainly

67

trousers, loose at the hips and upheld by a pair of worn and stained braces—for he was in his shirt-sleeves—detracted nothing.

She was at a loss for words. Then she began: "Dodds should have told you," and, correcting herself for it did not do to criticise her own head gardener before his subordinate, a filthy Bosch too whom it was charity even to employ, continued: "If you had any initiative you would surely see what there was for you to do without barging in on me in this impertinent fashion. You have no right to walk into my house."

Ernst now frowned. Amy noticed that he clenched his teeth behind his closed lips. She was frightened. Not a soul was within call were she in need of help. A show of extreme haughtiness was her best tactic. She would issue a command.

"Go back to the garden at once." He did not budge. He transfixed her with a piercing look from his falcon eyes, a look, not threatening, but disdainful.

"Gnädige Frau," he said, "it is, I suppose, under-standable that you should detest my nation, and me as a member of it. Although you are a lady it is not inconceivable that our situations might have been reversed. Some English ladies, voluntary nurses like yourself, as well as many thousands of English soldiers are at this moment interned in Germany. I am under the impression that they receive more courtesy than I am receiving from you." There was more than a trace of irony in his words.

Amy flushed darkly. "How dare you speak to me like this. Who do you suppose you are?" She gave him a quick look from top to bottom.

"I know very well who I am," he replied coolly.

"And who may that be?" she made the mistake of asking.

68

"Count Benedikt Karl Ernst zu Detmold-Ehrenberg is my name."

The hint of a smile as of a man who, with the minimum of hurt to himself, has knocked out another in the boxing ring, hovered on his mouth. Never, Amy thought, never had she seen a more personable and better bred male, in spite of his appalling clothes. But it would take more than noble status to impress her. The English landed gentry might have no prefixes to their name, but those who knew that they belonged to this exclusive and diminishing stratum of society often nourished an inverted pride in not bearing a title.

"Then you ought to be ashamed of yourself," she retorted. "A man in your position engaged in an unjust war which your Kaiser"—she spat the word—"provoked. And why too are you in the ranks, and not an officer? You would be if you were a true gentleman. I don't believe a word of it."

Ernst went the colour of beetroot.

"That, madam, is my concern. I am not bound to satisfy your curiosity."

"Well, get out then!" she shouted. He made a movement as if to leave, and turned towards the window. So he was obeying her peremptory dismissal. Had she been hasty? The question flashed across her mind although the haughty expression of her face remained unaltered. Yet an involuntary relaxation of her body reflected in the mirror was not lost on Ernst. He paused, faced her again and with a sweet smile which transformed his severe features, said:

"Then you have no commands to make of me, madam. I leave you to your English music. I am sorry you dislike my German composers as much as you dislike me who am working for you, by the way, for nothing and under the Geneva convention have no obligation to do so. You dismiss our Strauss, Lehar, Wagner, Haydn, Mozart even as so much dirt? You accept your Archibald Joyce. That seems unworthy of a lady of your high breeding and, if I may be so bold, education—and beauty."

Amy was confused. He must then have witnessed the whole undignified charade, from her selection of the gramophone record of *Dreaming* to her pirouettes before the pier-glass, which had been enacted under the blissful illusion that she was alone. He could not, had he been her own doctor or spiritual confessor, have more knowledge of her private, most intimate frailty. Unless he had actually seen her in the bath there was nothing about her she would less like exposed to this total stranger. It was highly embarrassing. It was one of life's cruel tricks. And yet—to be honest with herself—the fact that he was a total stranger, and an enemy alien was in a way she could not very well explain better than if he were a friend and compatriot.

Ernst had indeed witnessed the whole absurd incident from the beginning. It had fascinated him. Amy's furtive dashes to the side-board to attack the port decanter, her grimaces before the looking-glass and her dancing had laid bare to his vigilant eye even more than she imagined. Her needs were his needs. This silly grass widow had betrayed herself to him utterly. He felt about as sorry for her as a spider for a fly.

Amy bridled. "Your insolence is insufferable," she said with too little conviction. "I don't know why I support it." The words were some retraction of the preceding dismissal.

70

"I know," he then said gently. "I know very well."

"You know nothing of the sort."

"I think I know something which, if I tell you, may make you dislike me half as much as you do now," he went on in a voice more pleading than ingratiating.

"Nothing could make me even tolerate a German, far less cease disliking him."

He hated her for this. "If you suppose I am ashamed of my German blood, you may suppose anything you please," was his immediate retort. The effrontery, instead of rousing her to box his ears and turn on her heels, disarmed her.

"What is it? Tell me," she said.

He had a good mind not to, but he played his cards better than she by pocketing his pride with a great effort. "My mother is an English lady," he said.

"Oh!" she muttered, taken aback, "Oh!" Suddenly the whole fatuity of their situation was revealed to her. It was as though he had with the blow of a sword struck her so that her prejudices fell in a thousand fragments to the ground. "As a matter of fact," she said, "mine *was* German. But—" she halted as though to recapture a shred of that protective armour which for years she had clasped like a breast-plate to fortify her British chauvinism, "but she had never lived in Germany and died when I was a very little girl." She laughed nervously. Ernst did not laugh with her. She made matters worse by adding, "My boy doesn't even know it."

"Your boy doesn't know it. Well! You have to keep that disgraceful accident from him, do you not? My Emperor knows perfectly well that his mother was English. He does not disguise it from his children, you know. And when I have children I shall not hide it from mine."

71

Amy was chastened by this rebuke. But she thought, "How astonishing and unpatriotic it is that I should be listening to a German prisoner inside my house praising the Kaiser without my uttering a word of protest."

Ernst had not finished. Without raising his voice he went on: "Do you suppose your King feels disgraced that his paternal grandfather was a German? Which really means that his father was too, and he is himself."

"Stop it!" Amy shouted, "and sit down."

Instead of obeying Ernst moved across the room towards the little table where the gramophone was. "I feel," he said, "we ought to keep our sense of proportion in these matters. They do say, don't they, that children inherit more physical and mental attributes from their mothers than their fathers. If this is so, then you ought to be more German than I, and I more English than you."

Amy was so taken aback by this incontrovertible argument that she was again bereft of speech.

"Nevertheless," he went on, "I am German by inheritance. And patriotism towards my fatherland comes first in my loyalties. You are right to put those of your country first, but you needn't be so damned offensive in the process." Whereupon he leafed through the album of gramophone records, selected one and put it on the turn-table. Dumbfounded and incapable of preventing him, Amy watched the liberty being taken like a person hypnotised.

"Since we both like music and both have an equal quantity of Teutonic, and I doubt not, Norman blood in our veins"—he was paying her an oblique compliment—"let us play a good Strauss waltz this time," he said while winding the antediluvian instrument. "I don't think much of your Joyce."

72

He knew everything, even down to recognising London operetta composers. In his turn, but with his back to the pier-glass Ernst began tapping the floor to the music. From where she sat Amy could see reflected the curve of his graceful head as well as the direct glint from his black daemonic eyes focussed upon her. He held out his arms.

"Come along!" he said with an air of authority which totally eclipsed the initial subservience of the man at the window a few minutes before. It was she who was now impelled to obey. Amy did not pause to deliberate further. Having decided upon the hazardous action she would not repine. She did what she had never done in all her life. She threw her cap over the windmill.

Clasped within those young man's arms she danced, hesitated, reversed and clung to him, throwing back her head and laughing. He kissed her long, slender throat and she accepted the familiarity without a flicker of remonstrance. Her life had suddenly gone head over heels, leaving no room for reason because there was no future in its consequences. Amy felt like a nymph sporting with a god who had descended from Mount Olympus and could be denied nothing. Being divine, he would melt into the air whereas she, being mortal, would be left undone, an object for the fingers of scorn. She had always felt sorry for, and a little envious of, Leda and Europa. How could they have been expected to resist the importunities of Jupiter the Swan or Jupiter the Bull? She had never been tempted this way before. And now, this fairy tale count, in the guise of a German prisoner, was come to ask for the virtue of the beautiful but bucolic maiden, poor, injured, adoring, hungry little Amy.

The third repetition of the *Blue Danube* having reached a premature and growling finale the couple wobbled to the sofa.

"Another glass of port wine perhaps," Ernst suggested without the trace of a smile.

"No, no, I never touch the stuff—on principle," Amy protested. "What about you?"

"I never touch the stuff—not even off principle," Ernst replied. He took both her hands in his and gazed into her face so that she flinched beneath his hooded eyes. "I only want one thing. You."

"Well, then you may have it," she said.

It was not very romantic. Amy gave herself unremittingly. Ernst took her to himself in a savage frenzy. His libido, three years locked up, found satisfaction in tearing at her clothes, kissing violently her neck, shoulders and breasts, and making powerful lunges inside her. "It is you, you I have been needing," he cried as he was drained of manhood. When he laid his head upon her lap, she gently stroked his hair. "My darling," she whispered.

She did not watch him go. She did not do anything. For an hour she sat on the chintz sofa, dishevelled, her hair falling about her shoulders, her dress in a terrible tangle. Had an acquaintance walked into the room, the Vicar for instance, he would have been amazed, would have thought the staid Mrs Fiennes-Templeton had been assaulted, raped, ravished. What other interpretation could there possibly be? She gazed into space, her eyes focussed beyond the open window where he had appeared and whence he had disappeared. Within an hour she had been visited by a tornado. She was found one person and left another. The former Mrs Fiennes-Templeton was dead for ever. But who had taken her place she could not yet determine. Never never in her wildest dreams had she imagined such an experience as the one she had been through. Gradually she recovered her senses.

"Count Benedikt Something Ernst zu Detmold-Ehrenberg," she kept repeating to herself. Amy had a bad memory. It was important that she put that name down on paper. Could it be true, or had he invented it? She must in any event make a note of it. So she moved, stiff, shaken and bruised. She felt for the first time in her life fulfilled. It was true. Count Benedikt, Something, Ernst zu, what was it?—she had already forgotten, Ehrenberg, of that she was sure. Picking up a stylograph, a new invention with a horrid protruding bit of wire through which the ink either flowed in a pale blue torrent, or didn't flow at all, she scratched his name on the back of a bridge score. As she did so the prefix Detmold miraculously recurred to her. She then tore off the unwanted parts of the bridge score, threw them in the waste-paper basket, and folding the piece on which she had written, put it in the secret drawer of her bureau. If anyone should come upon it, it would mean nothing to him or her. If this count really existed she might one day trace him through the Almanach de Gotha. She did not believe she would ever see him again.

(12)

ERNST walked, not with his customary briskness, across the gravel drive and down the grass terraces to the iron gate that led to the kitchen garden. It was an afternoon of oppressive calm. The sun beat relentlessly like the burning eye of God on the parched earth. Before Ernst reached the kitchen garden he was in a copious sweat. He felt unsteady, almost faint. There was not a soul about, nor would there be, he knew, until the guard came to fetch him in an hour or so's time. Against the brick wall by the potting-shed was a copper tap encased in wood, swathed with a bandage of stuffing to keep off the winter frosts. Above it, slung on a curved metal rack, was a coil of rubber hose-pipe. Ernst turned on the tap, then stripped off his clothes down to shoes and socks. He showered himself with the chilly flow of water from the nozzle of the hose-pipe. He gasped from the first shock of the jet, then he held the nozzle above his head so that the water streamed over his thick black hair, down his neck, the runnel between his breasts, over his back and buttocks. He felt cleansed, refreshed. But he had not considered how to dry himself. In the potting-shed he found some empty sacks. The rough texture of the canvas against his tender skin stimulated him. He re-dressed in his sticky, dirty clothes. But he could not work. Like Amy he reflected upon the past episode for what seemed an interminable time, half leaning, half sitting on the wooden table of the potting-shed.

What had he done? What risk had he run? What reprisal was in store for him? He had not, he could swear on oath, intended any such thing when he presented himself at Mrs Fiennes-Templeton's window. After that assumed hauteur she had not so much surrendered without a struggle as thrown herself upon him, demanding to be taken. She was as avid as he was himself. The moment he first saw her dancing to her own image in the looking-glass he knew exactly what she was wanting. It was all as clear as crystal although she did not see it like that when she first became aware of his presence. She was a fine woman, still in the prime of life and though too old for his taste her body betrayed no signs of descent down the porky slopes of middle age. It was as soft and yet as firm as Rupert's. Ah, there were resemblances to be sure, and differences. The same satiny skin, and did he imagine it, the same sweet incense-like odour; the same clinging eagerness once the preliminary caution was overcome. It seemed indecent even to consider Rupert within the context of what he had just been through. That baby face. That haunting innocence. That delicacy of abandon, not to the flesh but, as it were, to the communion of the spirit. It frightened him to contemplate the love he had aroused in the son. The mother was old enough to take care of herself. Yet he had not seduced the first; and the second had seduced him. Yes, Rupert was different. He was dependent, artless, Arcadian. Ernst felt socratic towards him, not lustful.

When the guard called for Ernst they found him on his knees prodding holes in the earth with a dibber along a straight string for the planting of Brussels sprouts. He bore his usual manner of aloof resignation, but inwardly he was alarmed. What if Mrs Fiennes-Templeton had, the moment he left her, telephoned the camp to complain that she had been molested by him while all alone in the large house with nobody to answer her frantic peals on the bell? It was just a possibility although he judged it unlikely seeing that she was extremely proud and had been zealous in meeting his advances. Such action would not, he knew, deter an unscrupulous woman. But he believed Amy to be decent in spite of her absurd chauvinism.

"All by yourself are you, eh?" one of the English corporals asked. "Where be Mr Dodds?"

"He has not been here all day," Ernst answered, pleased that the guard should find him where they had left him in the morning, apparently hard at work, without the head gardener to see he hadn't escaped.

"Not here all day? He never told us he were to be absentin' 'imself." The corporal was both displeased with Dodds and pleased with Ernst. "Now that's not right." Had anything gone wrong he would be held responsible for failing to hand over the prisoner to the gardener in person.

"He told me yesterday," said Ernst. "I thought you must know."

Thus Ernst earned golden opinions which were duly passed on to the Commandant.

(13)

CORPORAL Samuel Pritchard, although he never allowed himself to have favourites among the German prisoners, favoured Ernst. He preferred him to any of the officers and far and away to any of the men. He liked him for his courtesy and generosity to him, Sam, and he liked him for being so infinitely superior socially to any prisoner in the camp, whether *Offizier* or *Soldat*. Furthermore he knew him to be in civil life a count, which nobody else who was not close in the Commandant's confidence had an inkling of. Sam had a healthy respect for the upper classes and could be justly deemed a howling, old-fashioned snob.

Ever since his conversation in the servants' hall at the manor with sister Olive and Mrs Staples when the former disclosed that young Master Rupert had caused alarm and despondency by being found in the pleasure ground after dark during the very hour when Ernst was absent from the camp, Sam had been a little worried. He had some cause since he had gravely infringed Army regulations by helping a prisoner to absent himself, the penalty for which, if discovered, would be extremely severe for Sam. Court martial and imprisonment at the very least. He had little doubt that the coincidence of Ernst's absence from the camp and Rupert's from the manor had been contrived, and that the two had met by pre-arrangement. The conclusion Sam instantly jumped to—in fact it could have been the only reason—was that Ernst had suborned the lad to help him escape at some future date. Sam was not a little surprised because he had assumed that Ernst was, if not content, at least resigned to imprisonment until the war should end. He dreaded an escape being brought about, quite apart from his own concern in it, because he was sure Ernst would never succeed in crossing the Channel and returning to Germany, and would be arrested and shot. Such a fate for his favourite would sadden him. He did not worry unduly about Master Rupert for his involvement in the affair could only bring him a minor punishment, like flogging, he being well under age for trial as a traitor. So Sam kept his ears alert to any chance remark that might be made to him by the Commandant about an exchange of prisoners from his camp with those from another, it being the Government's policy not to let prisoners remain too long in the same camp lest friendships with the guards should develop, as had indeed happened between him and Ernst.

Less than a week after Ernst's encounter with Amy Fiennes-Templeton Sam was alone with the

Commandant in the latter's office. Colonel Wagstaffe, which was the Commandant's title and name, was frowning over a fresh batch of directives which had just arrived from the War Office. Sam was painfully prodding with his right forefinger rows of stiff keys of a superannuated typewriter resembling the manual of some medieval organ.

"Bloody people in Whitehall. Have nothing better to do than inundate us with their daily shower of bumph," exclaimed Colonel Wagstaffe, half to himself, and half to his subordinate. "In South Africa we were at least too far away to be badgered by the buggers."

"Yes, sir. Quite, sir." Corporal Pritchard knew when it became him to express sympathy, and to what extent.

"This lot is the fifth I've received in the past fortnight. Even the Vicar don't proclaim the banns of marriage more than three times; and then on successive Sundays, not every day of the week for a month." The Commandant was a great one for exaggerations adorned with similes, metaphors, mixed and muddled, whenever he was put out.

"Yes, sir. Quite, sir."

"For Christ's sake, man, don't go on repeating yourself like a cracked hurdy-gurdy."

"Quite, sir. No, sir," said Sam, varying the theme slightly.

"Now you know most of the prisoners on this list, Corporal. There are some fifteen of 'em. They want 'em all transferred to other camps. Why they can't all go to the same, blessed if I understand. So much simpler. But will you be glad to see the last of this lot? Are there any others not on the list you would like to get rid of? Any bolshy ones, for example? There's no.

63 for instance. He's a real bugger, I always feel."

"No. 63 is, ahem, a nasty beggar, as you say, sir."

"Actually I said bugger, Corporal."

"Well, whatever you like, sir. I doesn't find 'im too awkward. I've known far worse. I seems to deal with him all right. 'E seldom gives me trouble."

"You're too charitable. That's your drawback, Sam. You'll never get promotion so long as you keep that halo round your head. Well, then, we'll keep him, shall we? Is there anyone you would like to see the back of, in particular?"

"Well, there is no. 82, sir."

"82. Which is he?" and the Commandant fumbled with the register of inmates. "78, 79, 80, 81. Here we are. E. Ehrenberg or whatever his name is. The cultivated chap who never speaks. So you've got a down on him, have you, Corporal?"

"Oh no, sir." The very idea, thought Sam. "By no means, sir."

"I always supposed you fancied him," Colonel Wagstaffe guffawed, rising from his desk to dig Sam in the ribs. "So why the hell do you now want to get rid of him? Had a tiff, eh?"

Corporal Pritchard's furious blushes would have been noticeable were it not that his countenance was a perennial deep purple.

"Quite, sir. I mean no, sir."

"What the hell do you mean? Try and explain yourself, if you can, Corporal." The Commandant had learnt after two years and more of being boxed up in the same stuffy office for hours on end with Sam Pritchard that, although often inarticulate, his views were unfailingly honest and usually sound, based on a shrewd, yet kindly peasant intuition.

"Well, sir, it's like this, sir. No. 82 is a quiet,

81

h'inoffensive type. No trouble to any of the staff, but he ain't popular with them. They finds him lofty. And the prisoners don't care for 'im neither, I'll be bound. 'E doesn't join in with their frolics. I jest fancy 'e might be better suited to another camp where there is other clever, edicated chaps like he is, and the blokes 'ere wouldn't mind to see the back on 'im."

"Very well, then. He's a von or something, isn't he? Can't think why he went into the ranks. Why they allowed him in, those bloody Junkers."

"A count, sir." Sam was for upholding the dignity of his friend, Jerry though he was.

"That's worse still," Colonel Wagstaffe observed. "I agree we'd be better without him. Type his name on your list. Put down no. 82 and strike out one of the others. Any one will do."

Two weeks later the Commandant was in receipt of another sheaf of bumph, which this time confirmed the names and numbers of prisoners to be sent to different camps throughout Great Britain in accord-ance with Colonel Wagstaffe's amendments. Ernst's name and number were among them. The prisoners about to be shunted were given two days warning without explanation why they had been selected. Ernst's sentiment were ambivalent. He was sorry his work in the Templeton garden was to cease because, being solitary by nature, he was left on his own for the greater part of the daytime, unmolested by the crass and repetitive badinage of his companions in the ranks. Yet, although no disclosures had so far reached the Commandant from Amy Fiennes-Templeton or any other source, there would, if he remained, always be the possibility of another meeting with her to which he would be bound to respond—the flesh was so weak—with attendant risks. And there would be inevitable involvement with young Rupert when he returned for his next holiday. He foresaw infinite complications.

So Ernst got down to penning on an over-decorated sheet of writing-paper obtained through Sam from the village stores, a letter of farewell to Rupert which he signed in the Gothic flourish of his princely Germanic hand. He likewise added his full title, surname and address in capital letters, not excluding the telephone exchange and number.

Old Dodds was sorry to part with him, commending him for having worked almost as hard as an Englishman would have done, and conveying his belief that the mistress would be sorry to lose him. Ernst drew himself up to say that since the mistress had not once condescended to meet him in the garden, she must be totally indifferent to his departure. He then begged a special favour of the head gardener. Might he have his permission, before the guard came at five o'clock to take him away for the last time, to walk by himself into the pleasure ground and by the lake in order to store up a memory of a place which, in spite of his captivity in distressing circumstances, he had grown to like and admire? Dodds saw no harm in this request. He never thought a Bosch could be possessed of such tender sentiments. So during the last half hour of his servitude, as he liked to consider it, at Templeton Manor Ernst strolled down to the lake and Flora's Temple.

The door of the temple was still ajar. The interior was as desolate and decaying as he remembered it. Evidently no one had entered since his abortive tryst with Rupert over a month ago. For there on the marble

paving were the tell-tale remains of the torch which
he had dropped when he first saw his young friend
in the dark and rushed forward to greet him. The
glass was in fragments and the battery had fallen on
to the hard floor. Ernst kicked both torch and battery
to one side. He looked at the Chippendale bench
on which they had lain. The mattress was covered
with dust and bore an impression as of bodies that
had been in conflict. The scene induced in Ernst a
profound melancholy. To come a month later upon
the undisturbed vestiges of a scene with dramatic
implications is to be submitted to a judgement upon
the part one has played in it. It is to suffer self-
reproach and regret. It is to re-live the incident with
the further torment of hindsight, the realisation that
had the prelude been different the finale would have
been different too. Ernst was, like many Prussian
Junkers, lacking in sensitivity but, in spite of an
inflexible manner, abounding in sentimentality, an
emotion he was always at pains to keep subdued.
In gritting his teeth he slightly projected his jaw so
that his mouth assumed the hard thin line which
made women abase themselves before him. He walked
across to the bust and put his hand into the hollow slot
at the rear which Rupert had described to him. It was
not very deep but sufficiently concealed that no one
would suspect it to be there unless they attempted
to examine the bust minutely. His fingers touched
paper. He drew out a small but bulky envelope.
On it was written in a round, unformed hand, "For
E."

Ernst opened it. A sheet of paper, without heading,
was folded over an object wrapped in cotton wool. The
note read:

Dear Ernst,
In case anything happens to me, here is a memento. Keep it to
remember me by. I shall never never never forget you. You are
my only friend, Ernst.
With love from R.

Ernst unwrapped the enclosed object. It was a little
gold pencil and it was inlaid with a monogram in
blue enamel. A pretty trinket. How had the boy
acquired it? Ernst studied the monogram. An F and
a T were decipherable, but the first letter was not an
R. He could not make out what it was. His mother's
or father's perhaps. Rupert could not possibly have
owned, far less used, such a pencil himself. Ernst
decided at once that he must not accept it. Besides
a *gemeiner* prisoner of war could not carry about
anything so precious. But he was touched by Rupert's
intention and the juvenile message which accompanied
it. He carefully folded the note and placed it in the inner
pocket of his jacket. He sat down on the bench. With
the gold pencil he wrote on the back of his own sealed
envelope:

Dear R., I cannot take your memento. I would be a thief. At
least I am not that. Like you I am a gentleman. I need no further
pledge than the one we gave each other in the shed. You will
know what I mean. I shall keep it. Have no fear, little R. From
E.

Having wrapped up the gold pencil in the cotton wool
and slipped it back into Rupert's opened envelope
he dropped it with the letter which he had written
inside the gibbous neck of Flora. Ernst patted the
noseless face. "Look after them, old girl," he said.
"Auf wiedersehen!"

85

(14)

FOR several days Amy's step was brisker than usual. Her movements were more supple. Her face, to those of her own sex who had an eye for such transformations, radiated a contentment not habitual to her. The matron and some of the sisters with whom she worked at the hospital remarked on a sparkle in her eye not consonant with the war news, which was grim, and the information that her husband was about to be seconded to the Near East. Pritchard was quick to notice that the corners of her mouth turned upwards instead of down, and the tight, disapproving lines about the nostrils had given way to an unwonted joyousness. She remarked upon the inexplicable change to Mrs Staples whose only comment was to nod her head first from top to bottom and then from left to right.

"Butter wouldn't melt in 'er mouth. She's that amiable that it wouldn't surprise me if she addressed a word to you next time she comes into the kitchen." This prospect had the opposite effect upon Mrs Staples to that intended. The cook was galvanised into action. She dropped her crochet work on the floor, got up and walked to the lavatory where she locked herself in with a loud clack of the bolt and remained incarcerated for twenty minutes.

Alas, Amy's euphoria did not last longer than ten days at most. It began to dwindle when it dawned upon her that she was very much in love. That the appetite comes with eating may be an adage as old as the hills; but the appetite only once aroused may be no less voracious. Amy craved for a renewal of that rough treatment which she received from Ernst and was pleased to call love. But how was it to be brought

86

about? She had not, as Ernst remarked caustically to Dodds that very afternoon, once bothered to meet the German prisoner who for months past had been working, voluntarily, in her kitchen garden, or even convey to him a word of gratitude, so great had been her dislike of having to speak to the man unknown. Now that the man was known, at least in the biblical sense, it would be awkward for her to make his acquaintance on the footing of mistress inspecting his handiwork in her garden under the proprietary supervision of old Dodds. Dodds would certainly not leave her side for an instant. And even if he were to do so, she could hardly propose to Ernst a further rendezvous. How and where could one take place? Her lot struck Amy as bitter. She was prevented from meeting a man with whom she was infatuated, a man who spent every day of the week three hundred yards from her own house by the proprieties, by those absurd social conventions which dictated what was becoming a lady of her position, and furthermore by duty to King and country. She shuddered as she remembered her prejudices which amounted to spurning with contumely and disgust the enemy at her door. Her duty to her husband, fighting on foreign field for his and her freedom, she did not consider at all. These thoughts were spinning round her head as she sat at supper when Pritchard walked into the dining-room. Prim and correct in her starch and streamers Pritchard laid on Amy's table-mat a plate of semolina pudding over which a skin of a peculiarly repellent texture suggesting that the substance had been boiled not in milk, but chalk, was visibly forming.

"I don't think I can face this concoction," Amy said as the corners of her mouth turned down and her nostrils gave a snort as in olden days.

Pritchard was quick to notice that more than the sight of Mrs Staples's latest war-time recipe was disconcerting her mistress, although she had no clue to the cause.

"To think of the Belgian refugees what would welcome a dish like this," she said with a studied tactlessness calculated to induce a revelation of the new turn of affairs which was influencing Amy's manner. Pritchard had over the years learned the fine art of scaling the heights of impertinence without quite over-stepping them.

"Damn the Belgian refugees! They can have it," Amy exclaimed with unusual warmth. Pritchard never remembered the mistress using such a wicked word before, not in all her days.

"Yes, damn the refugees, and damn Mrs Staples too!" Amy cast down her napkin upon the table-cloth with that magnificent gesture with which the adoring saints must have cast their golden crowns around the glassy sea, and got up.

"Oh, Pritchard," she then said in a voice changed from the terrible to the pitiable, "do you think this ghastly war will last for ever? Will things ever be normal again; and will food ever be edible again?" She forced a laugh.

The confidential interrogative encouraged Pritchard to air her views, which were invariably second-hand, having seldom come further than from the neighbouring internment camp.

"Me brother Sam gives it another twelvemonth, m'm."

"On what authority, pray?"

"He be very thick with the Commandant. Colonel Flagstaff did tell him that the exchange of prisoners

88

pretended concern in Whitehall lest the Germans might be thinking on an invasion. They is sending the criminal types of prisoner to more distant camps in the north, for safety reasons. If they invades then they is sure to be dispelled."

"Oh, are all the prisoners being exchanged then?" There was a note of anxiety in Amy's voice.

"Not all, m'm. But you've no doubt heard from Mr Dodds that that Ernest is one of them. Has left already. Today was his last in the garden. Mr Dodds says he is quite sorry, and even shook him by the hand when he said goodbye, which is going a bit far to my way of thinking, though he be a fine upstanding young fellow."

"No, I had not heard. Nobody tells me anything," Amy said slowly as she sat down again. "That will do, Pritchard."

"Thank you, m'm."

(15)

PRITCHARD had her own ideas why Ernst was among "the criminal type" of prisoners being ex-changed at sudden notice, or rather sudden as far as the War Office was concerned, for that ponderous ministry moved slowly even at the height of war. But she could get nothing out of Sam. He merely pointed out, when she pumped him, that he was a very insignificant cog in the camp machinery, and that all policy was determined by the Commandant, whose name incidentally was Wagstaffe. Her brother's manner of parrying her inquisitiveness merely confirmed her suspicion that he did know the reason for Ernst's departure. Indeed he did, but it was not the one she suspected.

The weather being fair and warm Pritchard decided one evening that instead of the usual knitting and crocheting routine in the dreary servants' hall with no view from the windows, it would be a nice change to go for a stroll in the park. When she broached the idea to Mrs Staples it was met with a severe negative, expressed not in words but nervous blinking of the eyes, implying that she for one would not accompany her for fear of being seen from the front windows of the house by the mistress. Olive assured her that Mrs Fiennes-Templeton would like them to enjoy the air in the pleasure ground. Since the cook would by no means of persuasion be induced to set foot outside the house Pritchard wandered off by herself. It was midsummer and the evenings were as long as the shadows which elongated the shape of the house in a jagged jig-saw across the grass terraces and made the stumpy chimney-stacks into sharp arrows of doom. The enormous tulip tree, a glowing blaze in the dying sun viewed from the corner of the house which she skirted on emerging from the back yard, arrested Pritchard's attention. The long, thin flange of darkness which it cast across the lake like some gigantic net, enhanced the tree's bulk and girth. Which of the Templetons had planted it, and when, Pritchard could not remember. She remembered the Squire telling her—unlike the mistress he liked to impart anecdotes when she was at her busiest—that it was the largest of its kind in the midlands. Certainly it was so prominent a punctuation in the landscape that one was positively drawn towards it. It seemed to beckon one to come and pay homage to its hoary virility and power to

90

augment its majesty as each year passed by. Pritchard was no poet but she was accustomed to respect all wonders of nature as well as artifice.

As she descended the third and fourth terraces she recalled that it was just about there that she had come across Rupert on the last evening of the Easter holidays. His face was careworn and creased with anguish. He was almost breathless from having run towards her uphill from, it could only be, the lake. Where exactly had he been? The walk round the lake was nowadays obstructed by overgrown brambles and laurels. He could not have walked the whole way round it. Besides the path led nowhere else, it being raised between the lake and a wide fosse, always full of stagnant water, which separated the park from the home farm, now under plough. On reaching the tulip tree Pritchard was immediately confronted by the temple. She had always disliked this building. To her it was cold, unsanctified, sinister. She had seldom entered it all the years she had been in service at Templeton. She was not adventuresome. It now occurred to her that Rupert must have been there when he heard her calling. This evening her curiosity urged her to go inside and look around. Her domestic training impelled her to mutter timid exclamations of disapproval that the room was so dirty and untidy. It called aloud for someone with a broom and duster. There were flakes of plaster fallen from the ceiling on to the floor. They had lately been trodden on, as though by the feet of persons scuffling. One of the benches had been sat upon for the mattress was all over the place, and crumpled. Her eye lit upon the remains of a torch along the skirting. She picked it up. An odd sort of torch she thought, and not one she had seen in any of the Stafford ironmongers' shops. On the nickel bottom which had broken from the cheap hinge she noticed the manufacturer's name and address stamped. Peering through her thick lenses Pritchard could only make out from the awkward lettering that it was not English. "Humph!" she said to herself.

There were foot-marks too in the alcove, in front of, and what was stranger still, behind the horrid grey head of a leering gentleman—she could only suppose it was a gentleman—without a nose on a pedestal. There were marks of fingers upon the dusty head. She peered at the back of the head which had likewise been tampered with. This was made evident to her by further finger-marks on the dust. She peered and she peered until she saw a thin slither of paper protruding from behind the neck of the horrible gentleman. She pulled at it and extracted Ernst's letter to Rupert. This was thrilling, a reward for her meticulous detective work. Pritchard took the envelope to the door and sat on the top step under the portico. It was still broad daylight. Adjusting her spectacles she began to tackle the pencilled writing on the back of the envelope. The script was extremely difficult to decipher, being written in a long, sloping hand. By dint of much heavy breathing, running of the index finger under the lines and laboured movement of the lips Pritchard succeeded in deciphering the gist of Ernst's message. "Dear R"—that must be Master Rupert. And it was quite obvious who E was. He could not accept the memento, he couldn't. What would that be? The missing gold pencil perhaps. Wouldn't be a thief. Oh, the bad boy. But the pledge in the shed. The Hun would always keep that, whatever he meant by it. Well, well! Pritchard issued a low exhalation of breath which was more a confirmation of suspicion than a note of surprise. She held the sealed letter up to the waning light. No, she would not open it. Nor would she mention her discovery to a soul, not even Mrs Staples.

Tears welled into her eyes. "The poor little man," she whispered as she dropped the letter to join the wrapped pencil inside the neck of Flora. With her handkerchief she wiped off the finger-marks on Flora's head just in case someone else might come into the temple before Rupert—it was unlikely—and notice them as she had done. She thought she had cleaned them too much so she scooped from the floor some of the debris and sprinkled it evenly over the marble curls of the goddess of perpetual youth.

"Them disgusting foreigners!" she said out loud as she turned and quitted the temple of infamy.

(16)

AMY Fiennes-Templeton was becoming very worried. She had failed to menstruate either in the middle of June, or the middle of July. It was now the 20th July and Rupert would be coming home for his summer holidays in ten days time. Her predicament was a terrible one, but she had not been backward in considering what action she should take. She simply could not confide in Dr Watford. He had served the family since her father-in-law's day and would be profoundly shocked were she to tell him the truth. Anyway abortion was so frowned upon as to be unpractised by country doctors. She could not bring herself to consult the matron or any of the sisters at the hospital for she had never allowed herself to be on intimate terms with them. Few of her neighbours were more than acquaintances. The poor old Tulkinghorns were out of the question. She imagined Pritchard to be loyal in her way, but she was an incorrigible gossip. Moreover, by talking to her about her predicament she would derive no advice, and what was the use of her sympathy? The worst worry of all was that she had not seen Joshua for nearly a year, so she could not attribute her interesting condition to her husband. Nor was there a likelihood of her seeing him for an indefinite period since he had, she already knew, sailed for Mesopotamia.

There was only one thing to do, and weeks ago she had formulated a plan in the event of mid-July confirming her suspicions that she was pregnant. She must pretend that Joshua had been granted very short leave, so short that he would not have the opportunity of coming down to Templeton. In fact he would not even be able to go to London where normally he would get in touch with numerous friends, male as well as those disreputable female ones he nowadays consorted with. He would embark at Calais on a troop ship, calling at Southampton and docking for forty-eight, or safer still, twenty-four hours only. He would be allowed the night off to stay with her in an hotel. She would have to arrange that a telephone message came to her (she could not very well dispatch a faked telegram addressed to herself from, say, Calais) one Saturday morning when she would be at home. She would happen to hear the telephone bell ring and answer it herself. This would require careful timing since the telephone apparatus was in the flower room behind the baize door which separated the front from the back of the house, and was invariably heard and answered by Pritchard. The message would come from Joshua himself, just arrived at Southampton. It would beseech her to catch the first train to that port without a moment's delay. In such an emergency she would throw a few clothes into a Gladstone bag, dash to the station and rely upon the station-master to work out the rail connections to Southampton. Naturally there were precautions she would be obliged to take then and afterwards. She would have to convince the servants and villagers at Templeton and a few close neighbours like the Vicar and the Tulkinghorns of the credibility of her ruse. The fact that every telephone call came through the village post office, that the name of the caller, and usually the nature of the call were known to the post-mistress who, unless she was serving stamps or sweets to customers, listened in and later regaled to all and sundry what she had overheard, presented a problem. In this case the post-mistress, who would know that no such call to the manor had passed through her exchange would, if questioned by some curious busybody, vehemently declare it. Amy must simply trust to luck and hope no one would have occasion to question the post-mistress. As for Rupert who in normal circumstances would never forgive his mother for failing to demand his leave of absence from school, he would have to be told that there had been no time to fetch him all the way to Southampton. Luckily troop movements were kept so secret that no civilian would know whether or not a ship had called at Southampton on a specific weekend in July of 1917. As for future explanations were she to give birth to a child, she would have to own up to Joshua and depend upon his forgiveness and co-operation. She could not think so far ahead. Sufficient unto the day was the evil thereof.

On the following Saturday morning Amy made great point of inspecting the back regions: first the butler's pantry, and next the flower room. In the latter she loitered until Pritchard went upstairs to make the beds. Mrs Staples was, she supposed, in the kitchen or scullery, but she was so deaf as well as dumb that she didn't matter. The fictitious summons to Southampton came. Amy tore upstairs, calling loudly for Pritchard, assumed a countenance of much rejoicing, disclosed her news and intention to leave by the first train, ordered Pritchard to summon the village taxi instantly and hastily packed. Since her preparations had been thought out well in advance twenty minutes did not elapse before Amy was dressed in her most bewitching clothes, bag in hand, waiting at the front door for Mr Jenkin's rattle-trap. Waving goodbye to Pritchard she told her to expect her return either the following evening or the day after.

Although during the First World War trains in England might be delayed, they always went. More-over one could, if one were somebody like Mrs Fiennes-Templeton, get the station-master to flag an express train to stop at the nearest wayside halt provided the line ran through one's estate. Suffice it to say that well before dusk Amy arrived at Southampton, where she had never in her life been before and soon decided she never wanted to go to again. In order to avoid the unlikely risk of meeting someone who might recognise her she chose an extremely modest family hotel in which she spent two dreary nights alone. During the sojourn she barely set foot outside the building. She remained most of the daytime in bed, reading a little, hankering after Ernst a great deal and concentrating upon the extraordinary anomaly that the child in her womb

would be half German and half English on both its
parents' sides.

(17)

AT the end of the month Rupert came home for
the summer holidays. His mother's severe reprimand which she had written him on receipt of the
headmaster's complaint of obstructive behaviour and
veiled threat of expulsion seemed to have had some
beneficial effect. At least he would be returning to
school the next term. That Amy was spared the
appalling shame of her son being sacked and the
embarrassment of what to do with him was no small
mercy at so dire a time for her. Certainly Rupert was
rather subdued and less buoyant than formerly. He
was noticeably older, more adult, better looking. His
face had lost the roundness and softness of childhood.
The contours of his cheeks and chin were firmer, more
subtly defined. Yet his eyes were uncommunicative,
as though unwilling to disclose the secrets of his
soul. He greeted his mother with a dutiful kiss and
Pritchard who was hovering at the door to receive
his mackintosh, cricket bat and tennis-racket, which
looked as though they had been little used, with a
spontaneous hug. For a second his eyes beamed upon
her, then relapsed into an inward gaze. He did not
enquire after anyone or anything, as he usually did
after he had been away. He evinced no enthusiasms.
Was polite, as though he were a well brought up boy
come to stay in a stranger's house, and not his own
home. Pritchard cast inquisitive, anxious glances at

97

him, yet addressed him in the old teasing manner which hid her real feelings.

"Well, young man, yer doesn't look as pleased to be back as we would expect. I suppose yer've been ploughed in the exams and doesn't dare confess to your Mummy."

"The results have not been announced yet," he said solemnly.

"And it seems they have not been feeding you proper, if yer shape is anything to go by. Bag o' bones is what you are."

"He doesn't look as well as I would have expected, it is true," Amy pronounced. "And lines under his eyes too."

"Nor do you, mother," Rupert spoke for the first time. "Are you all right?"

"Yes, I'm perfectly all right, dear," she said in a deprecating way. At that very moment she was suffering from acute nausea.

"So am I, mother."

"That's splendid. Then we're both all right."

Pritchard nodded.

"Have you told him where you've been, and whom you've seen, m'm?" Pritchard broke in.

"To Southampton, to see your father," Amy said. She had some difficulty getting the words out.

"Oh, is he back?" Rupert exclaimed on a note both eager and apprehensive.

"No, he's gone already," Amy said, looking down at her feet which were rather too large.

"What! He's been on leave, and you never told me. You never let me see him?" Rupert was accusatory and his face reddened with indignation. "How could you?"

"I couldn't, because he was on his way from the

trenches to Mespot, by sea, and the ship called at Southampton for twenty-four hours. I was only told the day before by telephone. I scarcely saw anything of him," she said, and tears came to her eyes. "A mere evening we had together at a horrid little hotel. It was a fleeting occasion, believe me," and she blushed. Pritchard was smiling because she was thinking that the postman brought only one letter from the Captain every two months at most. Rupert continued to scowl. He fancied it became him to do so. In truth had his father been on leave at Templeton now things might have been awkward. It would surely have meant no clandestine meetings with Ernst, possibly no opportunities of exchanging a word, even a look with him. Although secretly relieved Rupert was nevertheless annoyed with his mother for arrogating his father to herself and making him realise that he was a mere second best.

"And when shall we see him again?" he asked.

"Goodness knows, dear. Perhaps not before this dreadful war is over."

This dreadful war! Once it was over then Ernst would return to Germany, and Rupert would be able to stay with him in his castle. He had not worked out the means of doing so, his parents' permission, the journey; nor had he contemplated the possibility of Ernst's not welcoming him. Meanwhile there was at least the joy of seeing him this afternoon. He could barely wait to finish luncheon. When the sparse meal was over and before his mother had time to enquire what he wanted to do in the long holidays—Pritchard had already with a knowing wink suggested that he would not want to work in the garden again—he slipped away, across the gravel drive and down the terraces. Through the iron gate he spied beneath a large

99

drooping net, which formerly enclosed the disused tennis court, Dodds's dirty white panama bobbing up and down amongst the raspberry bushes. The hat was behaving like a white owl that had got caught and couldn't get out.

"Hello, Dodds!"

"Afternoon, Master Rupert," the old man exclaimed, genuinely pleased to see him. Sweat was pouring from his face into a white bowl of raspberries which he held in one hand. A bunch of desiccated bass dangled from the waist-band of his striped apron. "And how are you, sir? Pleased to be home, I'm sure."

"Yes, thank you." And where was Ernst? Rupert could not bring himself to ask direct. He hedged. He skirted round the issue, until Dodds began complaining that he had more work than ever to do these days. "Without any 'elp too," he added.

"No help?" Rupert was anxious. A tightness gripped his intestines.

"None whatsoh'ever."

"But there's Ernst?" Rupert forced himself to enquire, wide-eyed.

"Gone, sir. Taken away. Sent to another camp. And no replacement yet. They never thinks of the h'inconvenience. Oh well, we must grin and bear it. There's a war on."

The boy said nothing. The casual words, "Gone. Taken away" rang in his ears like a knell. Taken away! With head down he walked as one in a trance, back through the iron gates and down to the lake and the temple. All he could concentrate upon now was the understanding they had come to that if anything were about to happen to one of them he would leave a message with Flora. Rupert went straight to the bust. The noseless face, hitherto vacant, seemed this

100

afternoon to stare at him with a positive malignity. Rupert put his hand into the hollow slot and extracted first Ernst's letter to him written from the camp, with his hurried pencil note on the back and then the torn envelope he had addressed to Ernst, now containing the rejected gold pencil. Ernst had taken away Rupert's affectionate little note. Greedily he read his friend's messages. He was a little wounded by their cool tone and the refusal to accept the memento. At least Ernst's reiteration of the pledge and assurance of a welcome at Schloss Ehrenberg were some small consolation. But to a boy of fifteen the day after tomorrow smacks of infinity.

Having carefully learned Ernst's title, name, address and telephone number by heart he put the letter back where Ernst had lodged it. It was the safest place for it. No one would think of looking there and he could always return to re-read it when he felt inclined. But he took from its wrapping the gold pencil and walked to the edge of the lake. Since Ernst had refused to accept his gift no one else would have it. Least of all his mother. He flung it like Excalibur as far as he could into the brown water. With a splash no louder than the rise of a trout it glittered for a second before sinking below the surface. No arm clothed in white samite, mystic, wonderful, rose to seize it. With a leaden heart Rupert returned to the house.

Over the tea table mother and son sat in silence, each wrapped in his own thoughts. Amy ate nothing. She merely took little sips of weak tea. Because it was the first day of the holidays Rupert had been given two freshly laid eggs and a slither of fried bacon. Looking extremely wretched he toyed with them as though they were a medicine and not a delicacy. Amy, who did not know what the matter was with her son, was

101

vexed. Pritchard, who did know, stood longer than was necessary by the side-board, muddling up knives and forks and putting them straight again.

"Aren't you hungry, dear? I had these eggs specially sent from the farm for you. They aren't powdered, you know," Amy said while emitting a prolonged sigh. "Really the young are impossible," she thought. "Everything is done to make them happy. They haven't a care in the world. And they are discontented. Whereas we, upon whom the miseries of the world weigh, and whose hearts are rendered asunder, keep a stiff upper lip, and do not so much as murmur." Aloud she said plaintively, "Please eat as though you were enjoying your food, and look a little less like a wet blanket."

"You aren't eating anything either. And you don't look exactly hilarious," Rupert retorted.

"I don't have reason to be happy," she said.

"Nor do I. I happen to hate this war. It ruins everything," Rupert blazed forth.

"I don't see that it can affect you much," his mother said.

"It separates us from people."

"It separates me from people. You have all your little friends round you. It is we grown-ups who are separated. Think of me and your poor father, for instance."

"I have no friends," he said. And his lower lip quivered.

"That's a strange thing to say. What about all the boys at school?"

"I hate them—all," he growled.

"Rupert, it is very wicked of you to say such a thing. You shouldn't hate anybody, except the Ger—", and she left the last syllable unspoken.

102

"Well, mother, I do hate all the boys at school; and I don't hate all the Germans."

"I didn't actually say the Germans."

"You were going to."

"Well, I didn't quite."

"I should think not. I should think some Germans are far nicer than we are."

"Rupert!"

"I should think you do," Pritchard interjected; and under her breath, "one at least."

"It is very silly for little boys to air their opinions about life when they haven't experienced it," Amy went on.

"And is it still silly if they have, mother?"

"You at least know nothing about it, I like to think."

"What you may like to think may be far from the truth."

"How can you have the remotest clue to the dedication of one person, body and soul, to another, to one person's adoration of another? You are so cold by nature that I even doubt if you ever will." Amy was working herself into such an unwonted state of emotion that her own words overcame her natural stoicism. She put her head in her hands and burst into tears. It was the first time Rupert had witnessed an exhibition of uncontrolled grief on the part of a grown-up. He was disturbed and rather revolted that it should be his mother. He put his arms round her shoulders and likewise wept, not for her but for himself.

Pritchard was all agog. What could be the meaning of Mrs Fiennes-Templeton's break-down? Rupert's she could guess. But the mistress, so disciplined, so unloving, so indifferent to the master, well, well, well! She would have to have it all out with Mrs Staples.

103

Slowly she withdrew from the room like a stealthy panther returning to its lair, leaving mother and son in a flood of mingled tears.

(18)

IT took Pritchard several weeks to disentangle from the ravelled skein the meaningful threads of her mistress's unprecedented break-down in front of Rupert and herself. Amy's behaviour afterwards convinced the parlour-maid that something was, if not amiss with, then abnormal about her. Instead of her customary assurance and abruptness Amy displayed a hesitancy, almost a placidity of manner. Anxiety and apprehension were written upon her face as though she were pleading for sympathy and understanding. Moreover a period of lassitude and lack of appetite was followed by one of serenity and greed. Her very face and figure seemed different. Her slightly emaciated angularity had given place to matronly amplitude. Could it be that Mrs Fiennes-Templeton was going to have a baby?

Sitting one evening of early September in the servants' hall, her feet on the fender, Pritchard allowed the knitting to drop on her lap. Instead of rapidly flicking the tight loops of pearl and plain over the steel needle points her fingers, seldom idle, were busily computing dates.

"It were mid-July when the missus went to Southampton, weren't it?" Pritchard was really addressing herself not for the first time over this knotty matter. She nearly jumped out of her chair when the single word "yes" issued from the opposite chair in which Mrs Staples was blandly crocheting.

"Hmph! That won't do then."

"Won't do," came a muffled echo from that bundle of linen and bombazine, which was the cook.

"And not a letter from the Captain from that day to this. Absence don't esactly make the heart beat fonder. Besides, the processes of nature should take longer." Pritchard was on the scent of something.

"It were curious as how I were upstairs when the telephone rang that morning and you never heard it neither, although you was next door, having bolted yourself in when you heard her coming, and the wall of the water closet being no more nor a quarter of a h'inch thick."

Mrs Staples confirmed this observation by a perceptible sublevation and then declination of the head.

"It ain't as though her goes out of an evening, especially when Master Rupert be at school. There never were a lady what kept so much to herself, and never a gentleman to stay."

"Never." Mrs Staples was becoming quite talkative.

"Unless of course it were a secret rendy-voo." By this insinuation Mrs Staples was palpably pained. She raised her eyes above the half-moons of her rimless spectacles as much as to indicate that this time Olive really was going too far.

In thinking aloud Pritchard was well on the way to the conclusion of the chase. Moreover she was in possession of one piece of information which had for some time mystified her, but which she dared not impart to her companion for fear of scandalising that honourable and downtrodden lady. In dusting Mrs Fiennes-Templeton's writing-table she had taken the liberty of opening the little drawer which was secret to its owner and to her as well. On top of a small handful of letters from the Captain (which she would never dream of reading) lay the torn bridge score containing the outlandish names scratched in pale blue ink of some foreign potentate. Pritchard's eye was alerted by, amongst others, that of Ernst. Now no foreign prince had in all her years at Templeton ever stayed there, or been written to that she was aware of. And it was she who invariably emptied the oak letter box with brass-edged slit in the lid, to pass the morning's contents to the postman at the back door. Another shred of evidence which she had sifted came from her brother Sam. While discussing the recent exchange of German prisoners Sam had lamented the departure of Ernst whom he eulogised as a perfect gentleman and saw no harm, now he had gone, in revealing to have been a very highly born Junker. In an unguarded moment he let fall how, on the day when Pritchard and Mrs Staples, with other ladies of the village, had gone to Birmingham accompanied by Dodds, the guard had neglected to hand over Ernst to responsible custody, which it was their bounden duty to do. The fact that Ernst was still in the kitchen garden on the guard's return that evening when he could have run away was further proof of his irreproachable conduct in honouring his parole.

"And when was it we went to Birmingham for the day?" Pritchard continued in a dreamy sort of way.

Mrs Staples shook her head sideways which meant that either she did not remember or else that it did not matter.

"It were gettin' on towards the end of May," Pritchard declared emphatically. Mrs Staples gave her head a slight upward jerk which indicated that if Olive knew all the time when it was, why did she bother to ask her. "It can't have been much later than the 21st or 22nd," Pritchard resumed. And she started rapidly to count on her fingers all over again. "That's more like it," she said.

(19)

THE summer holidays were not a great success as far as Rupert was concerned. His mother still went every weekday to the hospital. She organised very few outings for him and the minimum of entertainment at home. One afternoon they bicycled to the Tulkinghorns for tennis but Amy did not play. Another evening the Vicar and his wife came to supper. Amy actually asked Rupert if he would like her to invite a school friend to stay, but, as she confidently expected, he declined the kind offer. The evening before he went back to school she became confidential.

"I am going to tell you a secret, dear," she said as she leant affectionately towards him on the sofa. Her eyes were bright with anticipation of his delight.

"What could that possibly be, mother?" he asked.

"I am going to present you with a little brother, or sister," she said.

(20)

TIME at Templeton Manor towards the end of 1917 was, if not at a standstill, then ticking like an old grandfather clock in need of re-winding. Slates were slipping from the rooftops, gutters getting cluttered with accumulated dead leaves, downpipes leaking and window frames calling for a new coat of paint. The garden outside the walled enclosure was disintegrating. The only thing quickening was the child in Amy Fiennes-Templeton's womb. Events in the great world however were not standing still. In October the Bolshevist Revolution took place in Russia to be met with the counter-revolution of Kerensky and Kornilov, which failed. Horrified though the upper and middle classes in Britain were by these catastrophes they did not realise the impact they were to have upon the whole of civilisation. On other fronts developments took an upward turn. The Americans declared war on Austro-Hungary. British troops reached the Piave river to bolster their Italian allies who had suffered a humiliating defeat at Caporetto. The British took Passchendaele, made an offensive at Cambrai. The Hindenburg Line was broken. General Allenby entered Jerusalem.

On the last day of the last February of the war, as though in celebration of the strikes which broke out simultaneously in Vienna and Berlin, Mrs Fiennes-Templeton was delivered of a healthy baby boy weighing over 8 lbs. It seemed to Amy when she read the announcement that these particulars were unnecessarily punctuated. She even imagined that mention of the child's weight had been printed in bolder type than the rest of the announcement, as though the editor were aware of her guilty secret and determined to disclose it by sly innuendo. Dr Watford was amazed that so sturdy and well-formed an infant could be two months premature, which Amy stoutly maintained. In vain she had endeavoured to defer its birth until April, or late March at earliest, so that the doctor, the servants, the villagers and the neighbours might take it for granted that it had been conceived during the fictitious meeting with her husband at Southampton the previous July. But nature, which can rarely be imposed upon, is inclined in her blustering fashion to get the better of the most ingenious devices of human beings to hoodwink their fellows, simply by following the unvarying course of millions of years' evolution.

Had Amy been a war widow she would have turned a deaf ear to gossip and insinuation. Having however established her subterfuge she would stick to it. And what might be said behind her back was not going to deflect her. But her husband was very much alive. Although she never failed to write to him once a week, as much from duty as affection, she confined her news to impersonal matters—about the estate, the farms, the conditions on the Staffordshire front—totally neglecting her own little tribulations, her health, her happiness or unhappiness, because she knew these particulars bored him. Of course she referred to Rupert in somewhat general terms, mentioning his school reports which were not very satisfactory, but skating lightly over his strained relations with herself, again a matter which would not interest her husband beyond eliciting from him a rebuke for her cold treatment of their son (as it happened Joshua's replies to her letters were few and very far between). And she neither told him about her pregnancy nor the birth of the child, whom she had christened Peregrine, a name signifying a stranger. She simply did not know how to broach this subject which, having deferred too long, she put off altogether.

In February of 1919 Colonel (formerly Captain)

Joshua Fiennes-Templeton, MC, DSO, returned from Mesopotamia and was discharged from the army. From the troopship which carried him through the Bay of Biscay he was able to dispatch a cable to his wife warning her of the impending date of his arrival, even implying eagerness to be reunited with her. He did not however mention what Amy assumed, namely that he would be passing through London. On this occasion the cable was duly delivered in the customary buff envelope by the post-mistress's small son at the back door of the manor. It was handed to her mistress on a silver salver by Pritchard dressed in a new uniform with freshly starched cuffs and a frilly cap and blue streamers. Amy immediately ordered a matrimonial bedroom at Brown's Hotel in Dover Street and on the allotted date took the train to London. She was in a state of great perturbation and nervous tension. At last she had to break the news that she had begotten a bastard child in her husband's absence. That he would at first be angry, very angry, she had no doubt. Any man would be. But at least the first explosion of rage would take place away from home on neutral territory. By the time they reached home together he would, she fervently hoped, have forgiven her, or if not yet forgiven, consented like the gentleman he was to accept the child as his and corroborate her ruse, that he and she had met at Southampton on his passage to the Near East. In fear and trembling Amy paid the taxi at the hotel. On enquiring of the hall porter whether her husband had yet arrived, and on being told that he had not, she took the lift to their bedroom, threw herself into an armchair and waited.

(21)

MEANWHILE the household at the manor all had their feet up. Pritchard having supervised the pulling down of blinds, closing of shutters, fixing of burglar bells, drawing of curtains and bolting of doors was relaxing over a nice cup of Lipton's tea and impressing the batch of new servants with reminiscences of her long service with the Fiennes-Templeton family. A fire was once again blazing in the grate of the servants' hall. The warmth thereby engendered and the wide-eyed appreciation of her young and inexperienced audience imparted that degree of complacency which is one of the few perquisites of the elderly. The cosiness of the scene was enhanced by a raging wind and the slashing of the window panes with rain outdoors.

"As I was a–saying we had double the number of staff when I first came. Things were done proper in them days. Up at 5.30 prompt, breaking the ice in the wash basins and burning one's fingers polishing the grates still hot from the evening afore. And the house-keeper, she *were* a sultan all right. She wouldn't stand no lip from the housemaids, not she. As for Mr Bankes, the butler, he might have been God Almighty. When he were put out and spoke his mind the young footmen were so frightened they did themselves a mischief many a time." Pritchard was holding forth with relish about these bygone tyrannies to the accompaniment of rhythmical noddings of agreement from Mrs Staples when a loud and prolonged peal of a bell interrupted the flow of information and caused consternation.

"Gracious me!" Pritchard exclaimed. "Run to the bell-board one of you and see which registers. Quick!" In an instant Nellie the new kitchen-maid having flown

111

to the bell indicator and back, reported breathlessly, "It's the front door, Miss Pritchard."

"The front door! Who could it possibly be, on a night like this too?" The bell rang again in a series of short, sharp peals. Without having time to put on her cap Pritchard made her stately way to the front of the house, switching on lights as she went. One of the girls followed at a discreet distance in case the caller might prove to be a burglar or a drunk. Stealthily the parlour-maid turned the key in the large brass lock and opened the door. A gust of watery wind blew through the porch.

"Who is it?" she asked.

She could merely see the outline of a human figure in the pitch darkness. A familiar voice replied, "Someone you used to admit readily enough into these sacred precincts, my dear."

"Well, I'm blessed, if it isn't the master. Come in, sir, at once. And to think of you on a night like this at your own front door." Pritchard was in such a fluster she scarcely knew what she was saying or doing.

Joshua was wafted into the porch, followed by a man carrying luggage. The Colonel was dressed in uniform under a heavy khaki top-coat. When he took off his peaked cap with a red band round the brim a laughing face was revealed upon a short, somewhat round-shouldered, gnome-like body. A pair of merry, darting brown eyes, a little too close together, intruded upon the bridge of a sharp badger's nose. The mouth was oddly baby-like and mobile. Altogether it was a friendly, alert face which strangers, especially foreigners, at first made the mistake of supposing belonged to a simpleton, a stage caricature of the booby squire. But underneath the apparent vacuity lurked shrewdness.

No man was less on his dignity. On the contrary Joshua Fiennes-Templeton was the very reverse of what his high-sounding name implied. He treated his servants in exactly the same manner as his social equals, that is to say in addressing them with terms of endearment, often by pet names of his own invention, taking them into his confidence and regaling them with long stories, sometimes of a salacious nature, and laughing so loudly at his own jokes that it was often difficult to make out what precisely he was trying to convey. Unkind friends deemed him a bit of a bore.

"You're looking as saucy as ever, my dear. Haven't changed a scrap for the better. Lazy as ever too, I bet," he said. "Now you'll give this poor fellow a bed, I trust. He's brought me all the way from Southampton. A hired motor. We docked earlier than expected. Saw no point in trekking all the way to London and down again. Thought I'd come direct. Catch you out when you didn't expect me. Where's the missus? Put that damned stuff down in the hall, there's a good fellow, and go through to the back. Pritch will look after you," he addressed the driver who was standing in the doorway with his cap in his hand at attention, the water running from the seams of his jacket on to his leather leggings. "And bring me a whisky and soda, there's a dear girl," he said to Pritchard.

"The mistress has gone to London to meet you, sir," Pritchard explained. "She will be that disappointed. She thought you was going to Brown's Hotel."

"Oh Lord. Now I shall be in hot water. Better give her a ring and explain. Have you got any food in the house? I'm famished, you know."

"I'm sure Mrs Staples'll prepare something for you, sir. But it won't be the sort o' dinner she'd prepare if

113

she'd been forewarned in advance, I'm afeard. I'll get one of the girls to light the fire in the smoking-room. Perhaps you'll choose to eat in there this evening."

Pritchard was all of a bustle. She beckoned the housemaid to carry the valises upstairs and unpack them, ushered the driver to the back regions and, having communicated the news to Mrs Staples and the other servants, ordered the Squire's dressing-room to be got ready and dinner prepared instantly. She herself fetched from the pantry a decanter of whisky and a soda-water syphon encased within criss-cross metal bands which she carried into the smoking-room.

"It's nice to have you back again, sir. And I truly hopes it's for good and all," she said.

"Yes, it's all over for me at last," he said. "I'm fed to the back teeth with war service. Shall be de-mobbed in a jiffy. But I'm a lucky beggar. Barely received a scratch all these years. When you think how many that used to come here in the old days are now corpses mouldering overseas."

"It's sad, reelly," observed Pritchard who was more remarkable for under- than over-statements.

"I don't suppose there have been many changes since I was last at home," Joshua said.

"Things goes on much as usual," she replied.

"And Master Rupert? It will be interesting to see how he's grown. He's at school at present, I suppose."

"Oh yes, sir."

At that moment a loud, plaintive cry from upstairs was audible.

"Sounds as though you've got a cat shut up somewhere."

"Oh, no sir. Why, that's your son, sir."

"My son? You said just now he was at school. Besides he wouldn't make a noise like that, unless

114

he's demented. He was fourteen when I last saw him, damn it all."

"It's not Master Rupert, of course. It'll be little Peregrine, the baby."

"Baby? What baby? Whose damned baby?"

Pritchard was so astonished that she wondered if the Squire had lost his senses after being two years among those Arabs. She had been told they were all heathens. "I meant Master Peregrine, sir."

"Never heard of anyone with that name. Why the hell does it live here?"

Pritchard was nonplussed. Very deliberately and slowly she explained as though she were addressing a small child: "Madam must have written that last February she gave birth to another little boy, sir. Premature 'e was. But such a lovely baby as ever you saw. Why, I told him only this afternoon that his Daddy would be coming home in a day or two, and I'm sure he understood his old Pritchard, though he be but twelve months old next fortnight."

"Are you absolutely sure of what you are talking about, Pritch, you old humbug? You aren't getting senile in your old age, and inventing tales?"

"Me invent, sir? I wouldn't do such a thing. Every word I said is the truth. I'll ask Mrs Staples to come and confirm, if you likes."

"Her confirmation wouldn't amount to much. Besides, of course I believe you."

Joshua scratched his head and gave vent to a whistle. Then he said, "Delighted to believe you. Well, I'm buggered. My missus has gone and cuckolded me." And he burst into guffaws of laughter. Pritchard was more than ever certain that her master was deranged.

"Cuck-old-ed me," he repeated the syllables separately while tears of laughter coursed down his cheeks.

115

"I'm sure the mistress never scolded you," she said, bemused. "She'd be glad to have given you another son, sir."

"I said *cuckold*. You've heard of the cuckoo, which lays its eggs in another bird's nest. Well, my hen has hatched another bird's egg in my nest, that's all." And again he shook with merriment. Pritchard, accustomed to the Squire's bold manner of speech, nevertheless knew, such was her training, what kind of expression it behoved her to assume. She put on her village idiot cum-Primitive Methodist face and retired from the room.

Pritchard was profoundly shocked by Joshua's reaction. That he had not already heard by letter of Peregrine's birth was extraordinary enough. That on learning the fact he should not be indignant but should on the contrary be amused was more than extraordinary. It was downright unwholesome. What were the gentry coming to? It must be the war that had done it. She could not wait to confabulate with Mrs Staples.

(22)

HARDLY had husband and wife greeted each other after their long separation than Joshua accosted her with the words, "Well, my dear, you seem to have found consolation during my absence. I hope he makes you very very happy."

At first Amy assumed that he was being caustic.

"I am not quite sure what you mean," she said in a hesitant manner unusual with her.

116

"I mean your lover. The father of the baby upstairs. I hope he's a decent chap."

Amy did not relish a spade being called a spade. She considered it common. Nevertheless she said, "I don't quite know whether he's decent or not. I scarcely know him."

"It does take longer to know a person than one thinks on first falling in love with him, or her. I mean it does take a time before one realises whether that person is a rotter or not. No doubt you haven't reached the stage of disillusion yet. It usually comes when one has fallen out of love. It is then that one is in a sane enough state to judge whether one has made a sensible choice or not. So long as one is madly in love one is living in a fool's paradise. One is insane, and jolly nice it is too. As I said, I only hope he is making you happy, old girl, pro tem."

"Is that all you hope, Joshua?"

"It's enough, isn't it?"

"Then you don't mind, dear?"

"Not a scrap, old girl. It's a jolly good show. I wish you the best of luck. Of course it's a bit of a bore having another baby in the house, all that howling and all those nappies and things. But the house is large enough. It won't intrude too much, I don't suppose. And we can afford it."

"Is that all you have to say?"

"What more would you like?"

"Nothing."

Amy was extremely offended. Anger, jealousy and the normal male resentment of another man having enjoyed his wife's favours she could have borne. Indeed, she expected to bear the brunt of them. She would even have welcomed them. But this total unconcern was too much for her to stomach. It was clear that he didn't even want to know who the father of the child was. She was about to leave the room when he said, while emitting that gurgling laugh which she now found irritating, "Poor old Pritchard doesn't know what the word cuckold means. I had to explain it to her." His hunched shoulders were shaking.

"You mentioned that word in reference to what I had done to you? You conveyed to Pritchard that Peregrine was not your son, but mine by a lover?" she hissed at him.

"Well, of course, old girl. Don't take it so seriously. She'll think it a great joke."

"She will think it a great joke. And so will Mrs Staples; and the servants; and Dodds; and the new chauffeur; and the entire village; and the Vicar; and the Tulkinghorns; and all the neighbours; and the county; and the whole world, for all you care. This is the acknowledgement I receive on your return from the war, I who have slaved for you, keeping this huge house going, bearing the entire responsibility for the estate, looking after Rupert single-handed, without one word of thanks. And what does my reward amount to? Humiliation. If you suppose I am going to submit to this, you can think again. I'm off." Amy swept from the room. He did nothing to stop her.

She spent the rest of the day packing her trunks. She did not come downstairs for luncheon. By the evening she had taken a train back to London having left a note for Joshua on the hall table announcing that when she had found a flat for herself she would send for Peregrine and the nurse. Having read it Joshua screwed it up, chucked it into the waste-paper basket and said, "Oh God, how I hate scenes." Then he rang the bell for a tray of whisky and soda to be brought to the smoking-room.

(23)

AMY insisted upon being driven to Stafford. She did not wish to submit to enquiries of the station-master and porters as to what was bringing her back to the local station with quantities of luggage so soon after her arrival from London. She felt utterly drained of vitality. She got in and out of the car like a robot. Hales, the new chauffeur, touched his cap in respectful manner which she could barely acknowledge with a cursory nod. A porter piled her trunks and suitcases on to a barrow and, directing her to the ticket office, said he would put the things in the van of the next train to London. Amy was so fearful of meeting a traveller she knew and having to talk that she bought herself a second-class ticket instead of a first. When the train drew in she forgot to look for the porter who, having fulfilled his task, was searching for her through the windows of the first-class coaches. When he found her he looked surprised, took off his cap and waited. Amy fumbled in her handbag, brought out a sixpence, gave it to him and said, "Thank you." She leant back in a corner seat facing the engine and closed her eyes.

The decision she had reached was so unforeseen, so disturbing that she could scarcely believe what had happened. It had needed no deliberation. It had been the spontaneous reaction of a deeply aggrieved woman who did not pause for reflection. A woman scorned is what she was, and what she could never forget. The scorner she would never forgive. Did it mean that she was also a woman with too lofty an opinion of herself? No, she would not hold herself cheap for any man. Somehow she did not consider whether she had held herself cheap for Ernst that July afternoon on the dining-room sofa. Was she being unfair to Joshua?

Was she making no allowances for the great strain, danger and unwonted responsibilities to which he had been subjected for four and a half years? Their friends would undoubtedly blame her for leaving him within hours of their reunion after the bloodiest war in history. But no. She remembered the dutiful letters she had written him once a week throughout those difficult years and the infrequent replies she received. And how distant was his tone. She knew that other soldiers' wives received letters regularly from their husbands at the front. And most of them were loving, so their recipients had assured her in the hospital canteen. And if uneducated Tommies, to whom writing was a labour in ideal circumstances and a penance in the trenches, could communicate with their wives, then certainly an officer of Joshua's standing could have done so, had he wanted to. She recalled too the unsatisfactory leaves they had spent together in London and at Templeton. She was made unmistakably aware that he was bored to tears by her. Their brief encounter this morning merely confirmed his indifference. It was the last straw. By the time she drove down Dover Street and her taxi stopped at Brown's Hotel Amy knew that she had acted correctly.

Luckily for her she had her own money. She could look for and rent the most conveniently furnished flat that might be on the market. She soon found one in that gloomy district south of Victoria Street which revolves round Westminster Cathedral. It was on the fourth floor of a gaunt block of sombre brown brick, striped with horizontal white lines like a zebra, called Ashley Gardens. The architecture was neither so outrageous as Pont Street Dutch nor so plutocratic as Grosvenor Place François Premier. The interior was embellished with a multiplicity of brightly polished brass handles and letter boxes attached to dark mahogany doors under *art nouveau* glass panels in yellows and reds richly dight. A lift operated by a rope wafted her to her own door, which was exactly similar to her neighbours'. After a year or more Amy would decide whether she wanted to live permanently in London or the country; whether she needed a house or an unfurnished flat of her own into which to put the furniture she already had in store and those other belongings she had contributed to Templeton. It would, she admitted to herself, give her no little pleasure to send a large removal van down to Staffordshire to despoil that unlamented dwelling. Meanwhile she would not communicate direct with Joshua in any way whatever. She would wait and see if he communicated with her.

The weeks went by and he did not communicate. She paid a visit to her solicitors and instructed them to open divorce proceedings on her behalf. This they did on two understandings: that Colonel Fiennes-Templeton would relinquish guardianship of Peregrine to his mother absolutely; and would commit adultery with an unknown lady in a Bournemouth hotel on a date to suit himself. Her husband's ready consent to the first condition and eager collusion and cooperation over the distasteful conjunction involved in the second amazed and offended his wife still further.

Although the baby and his nurse were soon installed in Ashley Gardens their presence no more filled Amy with unmitigated delight than Rupert's had done all the years of that boy's existence. No one could with any justification complain that Amy neglected her baby son. She was assiduous in her attentions to him. No mother could have been more dutiful. She

121

invariably put his welfare before her own and if he were the slightest bit indisposed would cancel any engagement she had made. Rupert would on passing through London visit his mother but could seldom be prevailed upon to stay more than two nights at most under her roof between school and Templeton. In fact he spent the greater part of the holidays with Joshua in the country. He had not been submitted to pressure by either parent. He had not even pondered over the choice. He had automatically assumed that his place was at Templeton where his easy-going father greeted him with a warmth which his mother failed to impart. With her he remained ill at ease. To her he seemed critical of her treatment of his father without ever making direct reference to their separation. By the time his parents' divorce was through Rupert was just eighteen years old, about to leave school and hopeful of passing the entrance examination to Worcester College, Oxford.

He had shot up in stature, as tall as he would ever be, well proportioned with an attractive if not strictly handsome face of the English white and rose petal cast. His voice had a curious deep, far-away quality like the bell of a buoy tolling out at sea. It was harmonious but melancholy. He spoke little. He was very fastidious, clean and neat. Mentally he struck strangers as retarded. In the ways of the world he was certainly insufficiently versed. He was abnormally unpractical, being incapable, for example, of taking the mechanism of a clock or car to pieces and putting it together again, looking up a train in Bradshaw, or even knowing what to say in company either to grown-ups or contemporaries, being so awkward in other people's houses that he fell over their carpets, broke their chairs when he sat in them and dropped coffee cups if asked to hand them round. At least this is how his mother described him to her friends. She would not say he was half-witted, but implied that he was getting on that way. His head was permanently in the clouds like a kite of which the string had escaped the hands of its vaunted manipulator, herself, and could not be retrieved. Because she had not a clue to what was going on in his mind she assumed that nothing was, and that it was empty. His father merely laughed at Rupert's vagueness and detachment. He was not worried; he was amused. In his happy-go-lucky way he recognised that Rupert was turning into someone quite unlike himself, the jolly extrovert host, the welcome guest who kept the tables in a roar, the good fellow, adroit with gun and fishing-rod, in fact the practical, insensitive but easy fellow who bull-dozed his way through life, deliberately smashing his path through fences instead of attempting and failing to circumvent them. Whereas he was wholly uncaring of the toes he trod upon, and in consequence miraculously wounded few, Rupert, who tried very hard to keep out of the way of other people's feet, was constantly tripping over them.

If Joshua laughed he was perceptive enough to see that his son was a thinker. He found no harm in his voracious addiction to Shelley and Keats and his deep but desultory reading, desultory in that he did not read with an objective beyond the decreed books (and those without enthusiasm) for his Oxford entrance exam and was no scholar. He recognised poetry to be the romantic fodder which Rupert craved. What did concern this affectionate but feckless father a little—nothing ever worried him over much—was Rupert's natural reclusion. The boy never wanted to meet anyone, old or young. And that struck

123

Joshua who was effusively sociable as extremely odd and unnatural. Why, he asked himself, did his son positively shun the society of his own kind; why, when the front door bell rang did he immediately, almost instinctively bolt upstairs to his room and remain there until the danger of encountering a visitor had passed away? Joshua could not blame Rupert—Joshua seldom blamed or rebuked anyone—for keeping himself so jealously to himself because he made his father's company the single exception. Rupert never tired of it, was wholly at ease with it in spite of their differences of temperament and interest. Their case was the attraction of opposites. The son found in the father his complement, the supplier of his own deficiencies, and the security he badly needed. He needed no other and liked to have his father entirely to himself. Since this was seldom possible owing to Joshua's gregariousness and their enforced separations, the father's rush visits to London and his amorous escapades and the son's terms at school, Rupert retreated further and further into his shell. In short Joshua was flattered by the exclusive affection he inspired and received. It did not take this shrewd man long to suspect that his son must have been, if he were not still, unhappily in love. But with whom? Or with what? That was the mystery. It would, he imagined, be revealed all in good time, not by direct disclosure because the most devoted sons seldom take their fathers into their confidence to that extent, but rather by what Rupert withheld from him.

(24)

Amy was neither happy nor content. Never a day want by that she did not reflect upon that glorious midsummer afternoon at Templeton when she was swept off her feet by a whirlwind which endured barely an hour and deposited her, as it were, eviscerated. She longed to be visited once more by that freak of nature. Her life was empty. She cared for nobody and nobody cared for her. She was intensely lonely. She liked to regard herself as a social outcast because she imagined that, what with Joshua's reprehensible lack of discretion and the gossip presumably spread by Pritchard among the servants at Templeton and thence to the village and the neighbourhood, the county of Staffordshire regarded her, hitherto a pillar of rectitude, now as a whited sepulchre, a fallen woman beyond the pale. Sooner than invite slights she avoided all her old acquaintances and never went anywhere like Harrods or the Army & Navy Stores where she might run into them up from the country on a day's shopping. During events like the Eton and Harrow March, the Motor Show or the Trooping of the Colour she remained indoors.

When she had hurriedly left Templeton she did not neglect to bring with her Ernst's full name, which she had recorded on the back of the bridge score and hidden in the secret drawer of her bureau. One day Amy went to the Westminster Public Library and asked to be shown the Almanach de Gotha. A pre-war edition was handed to her and with trembling fingers she turned the leaves. How small and insignificant the book turned out to be. Sure enough under the section *Génealogie des Seigneurs d'Allemagne* she came upon the entry of Detmold-

Ehrenberg. Her heart practically stopped beating at the sight of that name in print. There, prominent in italics, was the head of the family, "Benedikt Karl Ernst, 6ᵉ Comte de Detmold-Ehrenberg, Comte et Seigneur de Wendisch-Buchholz, né à Brandenburg 5 Mars 1892, fils de Wolfgang, 5ᵉ Prince et de Psse douair, Charlotte fille de Sir Richard Holtby, 9ᵉ Bart de Co. Westmorland, Angleterre." It was unquestionably her Ernst, the representative of an illustrious and ancient Prussian lineage. Against his name no particulars were given. This was to be expected of an entrant who was a child when this particular edition of the Almanach was published. Only the address of his chief seat of residence, Schloss Ehrenberg, was appended.

Amy decided that she would write to him. After all she had nothing to lose by doing so. If he did not answer she would be no worse off. On the other hand if she phrased her letter carefully, making no demands upon his interest, far less upon his affection, or his sympathy, yet discreetly alluding to the fact that she had given birth to his son and implying that in consequence (which was, strictly speaking, true) she was now parted from her husband and was expecting the decree nisi of her divorce to come through shortly, in other words making it clear that she was a free woman, he might be stirred by pride in having begotten a son (men were such queer animals) and a slight feeling of responsibility towards her, even a desire to meet her again. Amy with the utmost care, and after preparing five drafts, finally composed her letter to him in English. She began by conveying somewhat tritely how relieved she was that the war was over, how her sentiments towards his countrymen had been entirely changed by his just reprimands of her unbecoming chauvinism, how much on his account she loved their son, with whom she felt

126

sure he would be pleased if only he could see him, how delightful it would be to meet him again one day, ending with a sentence that made it clear that she not only bore him no resentment but liked him very much indeed. Having bought a $2\frac{1}{2}$d stamp she dropped the letter in a pillar box facing the west entrance of the Cathedral (the site of which in her ingenuous way she imagined might impart some numinous fervour to her veiled entreaties, for Ernst must surely be a Catholic).

Much to her surprise before a week passed the postman delivered through her brass letter box, shaped like a drooping water lily, a thick envelope with a heavily embossed coronet on the flap. Within a jet black border over a quarter of an inch thick, and under a German Republican stamp, were inscribed in a long, sloping script, Mrs Fiennes-Templeton's name and address in Ashley Gardens, S.W.1. Amy was so excited by its receipt that she could not bring herself to open it at once. Like a child who keeps the marzipan and icing sugar of a slice of Christmas cake till last, she waited until she had had her bath and gone to bed. There, propped by two pillows, she slit with the aid of a paper cutter the envelope and extracted a very long folded sheet, itself embossed with a crown above a steel engraving of Schloss Ehrenberg, and covered on both sides by spidery hand-writing. "My dear Mrs Fiennes-Templeton," it began. Amy sighed. He was observing a strict formality in spite of their intimacy of heretofore. In her letter to him she had evaded ambiguities by addressing him, "My dear Friend".

Although not once deviating from the dignified and courteous, Ernst's letter was touchy. It began with an announcement of his dear mother's death which he attributed to a broken heart and the conflict of her dual loyalties throughout the war. While openly espousing the cause of her adopted country she nevertheless remained an English woman whose inner sympathies had been with her native country. He, Ernst, had been fortunate in not suffering from any divided allegiances in spite of his English blood. He explained that it had been out of love for his mother that he consented at her urgent request not to receive a commission as an officer but to go into the ranks. For officers had to take upon themselves direct responsibility for killing the enemy. The *gemeine* had no such responsibility and if in battle they did take English lives then it was under compulsion from above. During the two years since his return he had struggled to encourage and nurse his mother in her illness, to repair some of the devastation to his estates as well as help restore, by assuming those public duties expected of a man in his position, the ravages inflicted upon the Fatherland and to mitigate as far as lay within his limited power those indignities now being inflicted upon her. He was referring to the newly established League of Nations taking over Danzig and the Saar district, and the Allies the Memel district, not to mention the inequitable imposition of indemnities amounting to hundreds of millions of pounds calculated to drain away the life blood of Germany. Over and above all these disasters hung the appalling cloud of international Communism which threatened to engulf his country and extirpate patricians such as himself.

Ernst continued his letter with the words: "But these evils are no more to be held at your door than mine. We both share the same dilution of German blood [Amy was not sure how much she liked this] and so can deplore the iniquitous reprisals being made against the German economy, not to mention Germany's rights [Amy felt a trickle of her old chauvinism reviving.

128

"After all," she murmured as she read, "*they* did start it."]

Ernst then went on to condole with Amy's present situation (a tactful reference to her divorce) yet to congratulate her on the birth of her second son who must be a great consolation to her during her tribulations. How greatly he would like to hear more about him. Whom did he resemble? His mother or his father? He had always loved children, finding it easier to communicate with them than adults, and wished it might be possible for him to see Peregrine (how beautifully chosen was the name). Hurray! thought Amy, she had touched that paternal chord which the news of the birth of his son arouses in every male. He too was lonely, what with his mother's recent death and the pressure of his duties which prevented him "consorting with [Ernst's English was correct, but slightly pedantic] *suitable* persons" of his own age (which Amy interpreted as young women with a sufficiency of quarterings to provide him with an eligible wife). Would not Amy consider paying him a visit, with or without Peregrine (the baby's situation was a tricky one, although Ernst was himself too delicate to imply it)? He suggested a date early in the following August, even giving directions how she should travel to his local town by train.

Amy put down the letter on the mauve bed sheets, drew down the pink silk shade of her reading lamp so that the light was not in her eyes, heaved a great sigh of satisfaction and smiled so that the corners of her mouth actually turned up. She had reason to be satisfied. For if she had been careful to make no demands in her letter, Ernst was putting a positive request to her in his. Even so there was a perceptible note of caution in the invitation. Amy had the sense to realise that if she were to hook this elusive fish she must tempt it with skill. She must give it a long line, allow it to feel that it had not swallowed the bait until too late to draw back. She must be patient, unhurried, and only strike when she knew there was no escape for him. Above all she must not show enthusiasm. So she waited a week or two before replying. In the meantime she made enquiries of Messrs Thomas Cook & Sons who worked out a detailed itinerary to Prussia for her. Then she wrote again to Ernst saying that she saw no real reason why she should not pay him a visit on the date he proposed, bringing Peregrine and the nurse with her. On receipt of a confirmatory letter from him she would order her ticket, but not before. By return of post she received a second letter conveying his pleasure at the prospect of greeting her and the baby, politely asking after the health of both but, as in his first letter, making no enquiries about Rupert. This she thought rather strange considering how the two of them had worked together for nearly a month in the walled garden at Templeton. She decided that the reason could only be that the absurdly proud man did not wish to recall those hours of his life when he had been in a state of servitude. She would not recall them to him.

(25)

AT the end of July Rupert left school for good. On his way home to Templeton he stayed a night with his mother in Ashley Gardens. Amy found his reserve extremely disconcerting. Try as she might she got no response from him. In fact the more she tried the worse she made matters. Because he suspected that she was pumping him for confidences so he withdrew from her. His suspicions which were not wholly justifiable made him cruel, as only the young can be cruel to a parent. He answered her questions in monosyllables. She learned nothing about his occupations, interests or ambitions. She could not make out whether he was pleased to be leaving school, or what he proposed to do before going up to Oxford in October. He made no enquiries as to what she might be doing during the remainder of the summer. In order to be left alone with him as little as possible she had bought four tickets for a theatre where they were joined by a couple of Amy's friends. To the friends Rupert was scarcely more communicative. When they telephoned to thank Amy next day they admitted that they had never come across a young man who made less social effort than Rupert and commiserated with his mother from the bottom of their hearts. After sulking his way through breakfast Rupert went into Victoria Street to hail a cab, helped the cabby pile his trunks and boxes on the roof of the taxi and, conceding to his mother a goodbye peck on the cheek, drove to Euston station.

On his arrival at Stafford station Rupert was met by the chauffeur and motored in his father's brand new Minerva touring car to Templeton. As the wheels crunched the freshly raked gravel of the drive Rupert observed his father standing on the steps by the front door to greet him. Joshua, with a greasy old trilby pulled down over his long nose, was wearing a pair of leather waders strapped to his thighs. In his right hand he carried a glass of whisky, in the other an enormous shovel of which the handle was entangled with weed. Dashing forward to shake his father's hand Rupert noticed how his jacket was spattered with the evil-smelling mud which he had been digging from the lake.

"Well, old boy, it's good to have you back. We'll have a bite of luncheon and then you can help me and the farm lads pull out that bloody weed which is choking the margin of the lake by Flora's temple."

"How ripping, Father," Rupert replied enthusiastically. He smiled broadly. Joshua throwing an arm round Rupert's shoulder piloted him into the dining-room. Breathlessly he embarked upon an improper story about the barmaid from the Templeton Arms being found with one of the farm hands, both stark naked in the hay loft, a sheep dog having run off with their clothes. The gist of the sequel was lost in a rumble of laughter which so shook Joshua's whole body that the whisky spilt from the tumbler he was carrying on to the floor-boards.

"Now, sir, I can't have none of this," came from Pritchard who was standing napkin in hand at the dining-room entrance. "Taking the polish off my floor and a-corrupting Master Rupert in the process."

"Corrupting be damned, you old B," the Squire retorted, while he continued to choke with merriment over his own witticism. "Why, he's so damned pi that I can't induce him to drink even a glass of cidrax in the middle of the day."

"And he's quite right too. If someone not a hundred miles from here would do the same the world would go round a deal faster than it do," she exclaimed.

"It goes round a damned sight faster than necessary as it is."

"That it do after you've had half a dozen glasses of that whisky, I'll be bound." Pritchard nowadays indulged in

132

chaff which would not have been tolerated in Amy's day.

"None of your sauce, old girl," he said. "You know what Pritch rhymes with, eh!" And Joshua subsided into his chair in a prolonged fit of spluttering and choking.

In the course of the meal Joshua disclosed what his plans were for the forthcoming weeks of Rupert's vacation. On the 11th August he would be motoring to Scotland for the opening day of grouse shooting with the Stewarts near Castle Douglas, then a week's September stalking with the Glen Artneys near Crieff, and a final ten days fishing in Sutherland with the Hamish Leveson-Gowers. At all these places Rupert would be very welcome and Joshua would love to have his company. But if he would rather not come he could remain at Templeton in spite of part of the house being shut up, most of the servants on holiday and the rest on board wages. Pritchard, he said, nodding his head in her direction, kept going off on holidays so often that he wondered she bothered to come back between whiles. Pritchard merely cast up her eyes to the ceiling with a look which plainly indicated that nothing the Squire said should be taken seriously. Rupert was not quite sure whether he would accompany his father. Might he think it over and discuss the subject again with him at dinner? In the meantime he wanted to find out from Pritchard whether if he were to go to Scotland with his father they would be alone together, in which case he might consent, or whether his father was taking one of those ineffable women, as his mother termed them, to his grand friends' houses, in which case he would prefer to stay behind. Two is company but three is none.

Pritchard, that inexhaustible and reliable source of information, confirmed that certainly one ineffable

133

woman would be joining the Squire at Carlisle for the first visit. She rather thought, but it had yet to be confirmed, that another might take the first's place at the last two residences. This forewarning gave Rupert the opportunity of telling his father over the port after dinner that on careful reflection he had decided not to accompany him to Scotland, much as he loved being with him. He did not care for sport and would feel out of place among his father's cronies on the moors, in the forests and along the rivers.

"Perhaps you're right, old son," Joshua said. "What will you do then?"

"Would you mind, Father, if I went abroad?"

"Abroad? What an extraordinary notion. Why d'you want to do that for Christ's sake?"

"Because I've never been there."

"H'm. A valid enough reason. You won't want to go there twice, so you may as well get it over and done with."

"But you were abroad for four years and more."

"Yes, but not from choice. I've had my fill of it I can tell you. Do please have just one glass of port to keep your old man company since you won't come with him to Scotland."

"Oh, Father, don't say that. All right, I'll have half a glass."

"Now, Rupert, you mustn't become a prig, you know. Won't do."

"I just don't like the taste, any more than you like abroad. But I admit that if I were obliged to drink it for four years I might acquire a taste for it."

"Yes, you might. You might also acquire a taste for some of the other good things of life if you only tried them."

Rupert blushed to the roots of his hair.

"Father, really!"

"We don't have to explain matters to each other, you and I. I mean, each understands what's in the other's mind without having to dot the i's and cross the t's. There's nothing we need withhold from one another. That's why we're such good pals. Always have been. Were before the war when you were ten and eleven. We don't have to beat about the bush. With your mother, for instance, it was beating about the bush all the time and never putting up a bird (he began to shake). I couldn't stick it. You know, I had only to cast half an eye over her the moment she walked into the house when the war was over, to realise that she was unchanged. I had hardly seen her since 1914—two or three times on leave only, and my God, were they picnics? A Salvation Army Commissioner would be more fun. I knew I had to take steps damned quick. Not waste a moment or a parting would be impossible. Then the good Lord gave me a trump card. She told me something that gave me the opportunity to turn her out lock, stock and barrel. May have been rather a cad, but by Jove, I did it, and ain't I glad I did?"

"Oh, I never knew what the reason for her leaving was. She never told me. I imagined she went of her own accord. Weren't you were rather rough with her, Dad? She was so looking forward to your return, you know."

"Um, yes, perhaps. More because she thought she ought to than from conviction, I suspect." For some reason best known to himself Joshua could not, in spite of his protestations to the contrary, bring himself to tell Rupert everything. About his mother's infidelity, for instance. Pritchard was an exception. Some people would think it in bad taste confiding in one's parlour-maid, but Pritch was such an old friend of the family. His own son, however, no. He just couldn't.

Then he remembered what he had begun to pontificate about before he was distracted by the mention of Amy.

"Yes, you mustn't become a prig. I'll tell you something. You're the best son in the world to me, but you need loosening up. You ought to fall in lust." He gave a guffaw.

Rupert said nothing. He merely fixed his gaze upon a small knot of black wood beneath the polish of an otherwise brown mahogany table top.

"Did you hear what I said?"

"Yes, Father."

"Well, then."

"Well, what?"

"Hell take it, boy. You ought to go to Paris and have a woman."

"I don't think I want a woman."

"You don't want a woman? Of course you do. There's no man made of flesh and blood that doesn't. Believe me. You're a normal fellow. Get yourself seduced, and you'll never look back."

At the beginning of this intimate conversation Rupert had also believed that he might be able to take his father into his full confidence and talk to him about Ernst. He longed to discuss the predicament he was in. "There's nothing we have to withhold from one another," Joshua had said, thinking he meant it. But it wasn't true. His father would be highly embarrassed and deeply upset if Rupert did not withhold certain things from him. That was the pity. There was nobody in the world Rupert had so much as mentioned Ernst's name to, no contemporary, no older person. There were certain topics one could never discuss with a soul. And ignorant, inexperienced, unintellectual though he was, he believed that his horizons were wider than those of the Squire Westerns from whom he was sprung. There was only one thing left for him to do. He must go to Germany in search of Ernst without further delay.

Ernst. Always Ernst remained in his thoughts day and night. He barely knew the man. He totted up the number of times he had addressed a word to him. They did not amount to ten at most. And on each occasion conversation had not been exactly fluent. On the last the association had been disrupted by Pritchard's voice calling. Besides he had not seen Ernst for over three years, but Ernst had taken possession of his mind, his heart and his soul. There was no room for anyone else, and hardly for anything else. It was lamentable but true. The nature of love was madness, even Rupert acknowledged that. Ernst was his lodestar. He became his religion. And Rupert was a fanatical disciple, as zealous and bigoted as a Wee Free or Plymouth Brother. He had built up over the past years an influence that guided his every footstep, regardless of its source which, for all he knew, might derive from his own fancy. The ripples widened gathering force day by day. That was the maddest thing. A pebble dropped by fate into a placid pool could bring about devastating turmoil to endure aeons maybe after the pebble itself had worn to—nothing. He was subordinating his intelligence to a myth. He fervently believed that Ernst advocated opinions that he had not heard him utter. He allowed these opinions to guide his judgements and actions. He fabricated standards of taste, choice of books, and pursuit of virtues which he attributed to Ernst's dictation. Thus Rupert would

137

vehemently deny, for example, that there was any beauty to be found in autumn colours, any merit in the novels of Arnold Bennett, any sense in the behaviour of his young contemporaries. He honestly and wilfully thought that he was echoing the opinions and obeying the prohibitions of the Messiah. A Messiah created by himself. Thus it was his duty as well as his inclination to set forth in pursuit of his God, to sit at his right hand, to pay him homage and to worship him for ever and ever.

"Then you don't object to my crossing the Channel. I might even walk with a pack on my back, might go anywhere, stay away for several weeks," he said to his father.

"Dear old boy, I think it may be quite the best thing for you to do, provided you don't miss out Gay Paree."

(26)

ON the 11th August Joshua after an early breakfast prepared to leave by road for Scotland. It was a clear, calm morning with a smell of incipient autumn in the air. Golden sunshine slanted over the tree tops. The lawns were spread with dew, the silver coverlet of which the Squire's spaniels had brushed in dark streaks with their hairy tails and stomachs. The Michaelmas daisies and phlox, still heavy with moisture from the night, exhaled the smoky-sweet scents which convey to man through the nostrils the melancholy reminder that summer is all but over. At the front door the Minerva motor, its hood folded down under a buttoned cover, was emitting pale blue fumes from the purring exhaust pipe. Hales the chauffeur was piling leather cases of guns, rifles and rods, loose rubbery burberries, tweed top-coats and basket-work shooting sticks on to the back seat, and strapping trunks and bags on to the luggage carrier at the rear. Joshua in a fit of choking laughter was issuing so many contradictory messages to Pritchard that she did not even trouble to say yes or no, sir. "Well, my dear," he said, turning to Rupert, "we'll meet in a month and more's time. You've get your money and your passport. Send me a post-card or two. Look after yourself. And don't behave too well." He broke into a fresh fit of spluttering and clambered into the front seat next to Hales. Pulling his trilby hat over his nose he submerged into a small bundle like a doormouse about to hibernate and was driven away.

"Well, I never," Pritchard exclaimed. "The fuss and bother he creates. He were never like this in the old days."

"I suppose he was different in the old days," Rupert repeated the last words in a ruminative sort of way.

"It's the war has done it. The war and the whisky," she said. "And the war produced the whisky. It's a shame, reelly. And now, young man, you must have yer breakfast, all in yer own time too. I won't be a minute."

Rupert wandered into the dining-room which smelled of half-consumed kipper, toast and coffee, the remains of his father's hasty meal. How different the room was to its transformation during the war. The round table was still in the window embrasure, but the long table had been brought back to the centre. The chintz sofa and armchairs, his mother's bureau and the accumulated bric-à-brac of a single living-room had been removed and dispersed about the house. The family portraits looked somewhat less disapproving than they had done during the hostilities. Generations stared stiffly at generations across the tattered Turkey carpet as though saying, "At least conditions are normal again, although *they*, our descendants, are a graceless lot compared to what we were."

Pritchard returned with fresh provisions of everything needed by an eighteen-year old youth, who begins with porridge.

"Do you still think Father will have a different friend at the last place?" he asked.

"On your life he will," Pritchard answered, and she pursed her lips. "It's that ball of fluff and tinsel, Lady 'Utchings, what he's picking up at Carlisle, to start with," she said.

"Pritchard, how do you know?"

"I knows, my lad, don't you fret. There's more knows Tom Fool than Tom Fool knows. Now don't let that there porridge get cold what I brought in for you special," and moving to the side-board she filled a large bowl, covering it with cream and brown sugar. She handed it to him. "Now jest you get on with it."

Pritchard showed no sign of hurry to get back to her pantry. She hovered, which meant that she had something to impart.

"And you be going to the continent, all by yourself, are you?"

"That's right, Pritchard?"

"I don't like yer to be alone," she said. "With all them foreigners about." She took off her spectacles and wiped the thick lenses with her apron. Rupert noticed how small and pig-like her eyes were. They were moist too.

"And where will you make for when you gets to Calleys?"

"I don't know, Pritchard."

"Oh yes, you do," she said.

Rupert looked up from his bowl. It struck him for the first time that Pritchard was growing old. Or was she just looking very sad? Before he could decide she came up to where he sat, threw her arms round him, gave him a hasty but fervent kiss on the mouth before he had time to wipe it and said, "Take care, my beauty. He's a bad 'un, he is, sure as eggs is eggs." Raising her apron to her face she darted out of the room.

Rupert concluded that Pritchard in a use of the third person singular was in her chauvinistic way referring to all foreigners in general. It did not occur to him that she could possibly have Ernst in mind. She had never mentioned Ernst's name since the day he left Templeton three years ago.

Rupert did not walk with a pack on his back. He acquired the best and most expensive bicycle that his indulgent father's allowance enabled him to buy in Stafford's main street. He bought a bright yellow outfit of synthetic rubber which smelled of fish and seaweed, with a hood to cover his head, and leggings his nether limbs in the event of rain. After scrupulous computation he reduced his luggage to the bare minimum. He furnished himself with several maps and Palgrave's *Golden Treasury* for reading. He would be so exhausted at the end of each day that he would need no other books. Within two days of his father's departure he set forth in very different circumstances. He was going to ride all the way to Prussia, crossing the sea by the shortest route. The whole staff assembled on the steps of the portico to see him off. There was old Dodds in his bleached panama, Mrs Staples in floods of tears, the new housemaids (they had been in service at the manor only two years)

141

and the kitchen maid in print dresses, with Pritchard in the centre of the group. They waved him goodbye, calling, "Good luck, Master Rupert!" and "God be with you!" Only Pritchard did not wave or say a word. At the end of the straight bit of drive before turning to the left by the great holm oak Rupert looked back. Dodds and the maids had disappeared. Pritchard alone remained, her hands to her brow, straining her myopic eyes to catch a last glimpse of him before he was lost to her. And he had not even kissed her, not liking to be seen doing so in front of the others.

He rode to Rugeley, and Lichfield and Nuneaton, avoiding the commercial towns, Walsall, Birmingham and Coventry. He stayed in wayside pubs and farm houses, some of the homely occupants of which did not want to charge the young gentleman with the earnest eyes and sweet expression. One farmer's wife said to her sister that he resembled a medieval saint on a pilgrimage to the Holy Land. But Prussia was his goal, not Jerusalem. He rode past Banbury, and Bicester and Thame. He avoided Oxford because he was due there in October and foolishly imagined he might be recognised by some contemptuous don who would turn out to be his tutor when he reached the university. He slept at Henley. He skirted London because it was too big and his mother would disapprove of his bicycle, and would ask tiresome questions, if he were to call at Ashley Gardens. From Windsor he struck south for Guildford where he set his face due east. He kept to the lanes below the North Downs, entering the Weald of Kent, emerging at Maidstone, crossing the Medway and making for Canterbury. The bells of the cathedral kept him awake at night. From Canterbury to Dover was a short hop. He had got his wind.

From Calais he bicycled through West and East Flanders and was sickened by the desolation he witnessed, the broken trees, the battered churches, the unfilled trenches, the occasional remnant of rifle and helmet sticking out of the ground in anguished protest. He pedalled through Belgium and South Brabant. From Holland he entered Germany. He kept north of the industrial zone of the Saar, passing through Hanover until he reached the flat, dull, endless Northern European Plain. On and on he went, not daring to rest for more than a night lest on relaxing he might not feel capable of resuming the pilgrimage. He covered fifty, sixty and even seventy miles a day. He dropped south into the Altmark, touching Northern Saxony, crossing the Elbe and finally reaching Brandenburg. Here he was within ten miles or so of his goal. He stopped for two nights in a wayside *gasthaus* of the old, walled city on the river Havel, ate an enormous German meal, explained to the host where he had come from on his bicycle, drank pints of beer, and slept for twenty-four hours. When he woke up he felt more exhausted than when he went to sleep, and stiff and aching in every limb. Moreover the weather had broken.

On the afternoon of his third day in Brandenburg he set off on the last short lap of the journey. He did not telephone to Schloss Ehrenberg to announce his arrival. His German was inadequate. He funked explaining to a servant who he was and being shrugged off by an excuse which would make it impossible for him to approach the castle afterwards. Besides Ernst might not be at home. He would take his chance and turn up unheralded.

Under a heavily laden sky Rupert bicycled across a sandy plain occasionally relieved by fertile fields of barley and rye, enclosures of sheep and innumerable little lakes. After two hours of pedalling through flat country there loomed at the far end of a straight and narrow road what in hilly country would be deemed an insignificant hump, clothed in spiky fir trees and dominated by a castle with keep and turrets. His map informed him that it was Schloss Ehrenberg.

Rupert finding himself after weeks of laborious travel within sight of his Holy Grail was overcome by nerves and shyness. Why had he undertaken such a stupid expedition? Why should he suppose that after three years the noble proprietor of this little principality would remember the circumstances of their distant friendship with any emotion but distaste? Would he remember him at all? The pledge in the potting-shed. How childish it all seemed now. On the other hand how could he, actually within sight of the goal, turn back? That would be even more absurd.

Then it started to rain. In order to look respectable on arrival Rupert had, before leaving the *gasthaus*, changed out of his old slacks and put on his clean shirt and best grey flannel suit. Under the shelter of a tree he was obliged to don the yellow rubber outfit, hood, leggings and the sheet which stretched over his arms to the handle-bars.

On approaching the hump Rupert bicycled through a small village of straggling low houses set back from the road with few flowers in the gardens save some drooping petunias and bedraggled sunflowers. At the end of the wide street where the road took a kink to the right towards Anhalt an untidy castellated lodge stood beside a pair of wide-open iron gates, one of which had come off its hinges. Rupert dismounted and pushed his bicycle up a long curving drive. Although from a distance the hump which this castle crowned

144

seemed a mere pimple on the landscape, it grew as he climbed. At last he reached the summit. A gap in the trees opened upon a level of shaggy lawn sprouting couch-grass, plantains and daisies. He was confronted by a high, nineteenth-century fortress of sombre brown stone, with narrow windows piercing the facade as it were at random, mansard roofs jutting ineptly from turrets and a *porte-cochère* large enough to shelter a travelling carriage and two pairs of horses. Not a gardener, not a servitor was to be seen on this gloomy afternoon. Having reached the forbidding entrance Rupert debated with himself whether to strip off his ungainly yellow outfit on the cobbles before ringing the bell, or ring the bell and enter the house as he was, the synthetic rubber dripping pools of water on the floor of a marble hall. He decided that, were he to be told that the Count was away and were he to be refused admittance, the ignominy of dressing up again would be worse than entering clad as he was. Summoning his courage he pulled a rusted iron bell-handle which emitted an indignant screech from the ratchet above it, and waited.

He waited. A moist wind blew a gust of soggy leaves round his feet. Rupert would have given anything he possessed, anything not to be where he was. Yet he gave a second tug at the bell. The screech from the ratchet repeated itself. He waited. A muffled sound of slow footsteps on the gravel approached, and an old bent man wearing green livery with embossed silver buttons hobbled towards him under a large mushroom umbrella. "Was wollen Sie?" he asked in a cracked voice. "Ist der Herr Graf zu Hause?" Rupert countered haltingly. "Ja," answered the old man; "aber was wünschen Sie?" "Ich möchte ihn. Ich bin seiner Freund, aus England," Rupert said. "Aus England," the old man repeated, amazed, and casting a suspicious glance from the dripping yellow apparition before him to the mud-caked bicycle propped against a column of the portico. After a moment's hesitation the servant continued, "Bitte, kommen Sie mir," and stumped off under the mushroom umbrella which he did not offer to share with the stranger from England.

Rupert was conducted through a Gothic archway to an enclosed courtyard. From the back door of the castle he was ushered into a bare little room furnished with an oak table and benches where he supposed the tenants and other petitioners were wont to assemble. It was made obvious that he was not the sort of visitor to be admitted by a posse of liveried footmen through the front door.

"Ihr Name, bitte?" the old man asked, not im-politely, but coldly.

"Herr von Fiennes-Templeton," Rupert said with a touch of arrogance.

"Was?"

"Never mind. Just say a friend from England." The name was clearly too complicated for registration. The old servant wandered off to inform a footman that a bedraggled young foreigner in the back premises craved the privilege of an audience with the Count.

"What, on an evening like this?" the footman enquired. "And where is his automobile?"

"He has arrived on a velocipede, and he is dressed like a man from the moon," said the old servant who had never travelled as far as Berlin.

"By velocipede I presume you imply a common or garden bicycle," the footman remarked in a lofty tone. He went in search of the Groom of the Chambers.

Since the numerous servants at Castle Ehrenberg were trained, like all high class servants the world over, not to knock on doors, the Groom of the Chambers, also dressed in green livery but with gold embossed buttons, rattled rather noisily on the library folding doors before turning a handle. Once inside the room he prefaced his annoucement with a loud *ahem*. The master was sprawling in a Byronic attitude on the hearth rug before fireplace at the far end of the room. By his side a lady was reclining, her back to the door, on a high-winged sofa.

"What is it, Johann?" Ernst asked without rising.

"There is a foreigner to see you, Herr Graf, on urgent business."

"Who is he? And where is he?"

"He has an unpronounceable name, Herr Graf, and he is at present in the audit chamber. He has come, not in an automobile, but on a velocipede."

"Oh, do let's see the foreigner with an unpronounceable name," the lady said in English. "He can't be the rate- or tax-collector or anyone horrid like that."

"Very well, show him in, Johann."

That high dignitary gravitated to the back regions like Lucifer condescending to fall from heaven. He whispered to the superior footman who nodded. The latter found Rupert in the poky little room by the back door, denominated the audit chamber, still enveloped in his yellow outfit from which the rain water was dripping pools on to the linoleum floor.

"The Count will receive you in the library," the footman declared as though he were a chamberlain addressing a bus-load of trippers from Saskatchewan about to be granted an audience of the Pope. "But you must take off those things first," he said in German, indicating the synthetic rubber.

Rupert peeled off the yellow accoutrement and left it in a pile on the bench. The footman with finger

147

and thumb gingerly picked up each piece in turn and dropped it on the floor. "Folgen Sie mir," he ordered.

Revealed in his best grey flannel suit Rupert recovered some confidence. He even impressed the superior footman who gave him an approving glance before leading the way through a maze of stone passages with thick pipes suspended from vaulted ceilings. They climbed a spiral staircase which debouched upon a carpeted corridor. Rupert was struck by the contrast of the opulent front of the house with the prison-like atmosphere of the servants' quarters below. The furniture of the corridor and ante-chambers through which they passed was expensive if not all of impeccable quality and taste. Boulle cabinets and Louis XVI commodes inlaid with porcelain plaques jostled with sub-Biedermeier cupboards and tables made fusty by the multi-coloured Turkish bazaar rugs which draped them. Full-length ancestors in armour brandishing swords against velvet curtains, with a puff of cannon smoke in the background, hung between horns of bison and elk. Elephant tusks and twisted narwhal horns stood sentinel at doorways, the brass handles of which were tightly gloved in suede. On a flimsy fretwork shelf a superlative pair of Meissen red stoneware vases reposed below the stuffed head of a rhinoceros, one of whose glass eyes dangled perilously from its socket. A grand piano, draped with a Venetian shawl, supported a forest of silver photograph frames and oleographs of Bismarck and the Emperor William II. Several windows and even doors they passed were opaquely glazed with stained figures of medieval knights and saints in every colour of the rainbow.

At the library door the footman halted. Pulling back the tapestry *portière* with his left hand and turning the gloved handle of one of the valves with his right he whispered, "Treten Sie durch! Der Herr Graf ist herein." And he closed the door softly behind him.

Rupert stood on a deep Savonnerie carpet at the far end of a long tunnel-like room. He was in shadow. On either side of him stretched two long ranges of books from floor to ceiling. The closely packed shelves of brown morocco bindings were broken by a horizontal gallery with a brightly gilded balustrade giving access to upper shelves containing smaller volumes. Quarter-length portraits of pacific ancestors were hung on red tasselled ropes above the books. Rupert looked about him. He thought he had never entered a more sumptuous yet cosy apartment. Scanty daylight percolated through two long casemented windows on either side of the fireplace, an elaborate confection of red veined marble. A small fire flickered in the grate. At first Rupert imagined he was alone in the room. Had the superior footman played a trick on him? Then from the hearth rug, from which he had not stirred since the Groom of the Chambers' original announcement, the master of the house rose to his feet. Against the light the slim silhouette was instantly recognisable to Rupert as Ernst's.

"Wie geht es Ihnen, mein Herr? Und sprechen Sie Deutsch?" the Count asked courteously as he advanced to meet the unknown visitor.

"I only speak a little German," Rupert answered in his bashful voice.

Ernst halted abruptly, resting one hand on a table of books and papers.

"You do not remember me?" Rupert remained where he was by the door. There was no reply. Then he held out both his hands. "Oh, Ernst," he said, "you told me I might come at any time." All doubts, hesitations, inhibitions dropped from him like

149

those cumbersome, protective garments in the audit chamber downstairs. He felt as untrammelled, naked and innocent as Adam before the Fall. Darting forward he impulsively clasped his friend in his arms. Laying his head on the other's shoulder he lightly brushed his smooth cheek with his own. "Oh Ernst, I simply had to come," he said.

Without returning the pressure Ernst calmly disengaged himself and stepping back held the boy at arms' length. Now at close quarters Rupert was able to look at him. Facially there was very little change: the same proud carriage of the head, the same thick black hair, now it is true, neatly parted and the natural waves smarmed down by a pomade; the same falcon's eyes rimmed with that ochre light beneath the same slanting brows; the same straight nose and severe mouth. But the whole outward mien was different. Gone of course the old stained grey jacket, baggy trousers and worn boots. The Count was immaculately apparelled in leather coat, green like his servants' livery, but with black braided edges, horn buttons, frogged button-holes and turned cuffs. A white silk handkerchief glistened from the breast pocket. A pair of nut brown brogues, highly polished, adorned his shapely feet.

Ernst was taken by complete surprise. His reaction was that of a man acutely disconcerted by the unwelcome reminder of a past misdeed. For a moment his sophistication was unable to cope with the situation. He managed to bring out the words, "It's Rupert. What an unexpected pleasure. And what brings you here?" The staccato words fell like a douche of cold water upon the unbidden guest.

"I believe you aren't pleased to see me," Rupert stammered. He was almost in tears. "I oughtn't to have come. You have forgotten the pledge, that we were to love one another for ever. You promised faithfully. I have never forgotten you, not for a single day. Never forgotten that we belong to one another." And he subsided on to a small cane chair, clutching the frail back of it.

Ernst remained standing at a distance. He was very straight, stiff and his face was expressionless.

A log in the fireplace slipped, spluttered and spurted forth a livid blue flame. Ernst recovered his sang-froid. His voice assumed a heartiness which belied any tenderness implicit in that word. On the contrary it had a sharp and hollow ring as of an axe against live wood.

"My poor boy, you are a little over-wrought after your long journey. I gather you have come on a bicycle. You must be worn out. What a pity you did not give me warning in advance." He retreated to the fireplace. Then almost truculently he said, "There is someone here to whom I need not introduce you. Your mother."

After a pause, "Darling," he went on, and there was an icy edge to the term which cut Rupert to the quick so that he gasped like one who has been thrown into a mountain torrent, "here is your son." With an affected gesture seldom witnessed in real life, but often employed by ham actors of eighteenth-century plays, he indicated the presence of Amy ensconced within the high back and arms of the sofa.

"Well, aren't you going to greet your mother?" Amy asked with maddening placidity. She did not stir from her slouching posture. Rupert detected disdain in her manner and a hint of triumph in her tone. Then, as though rising from the sawdust after being knocked out in a boxing-ring, he staggered across to his mother's seat, bent down and, speaking not a

151

word, undemonstratively kissed her. There was ice on his lips too.

For a minute the three remained in absolute silence. Neither Ernst nor Rupert had for the moment anything further to say. Amy was the first to break the deadlock for in the unwonted circumstances she held the uppermost hand.

"And what, I beg to be told, is the meaning of this extraordinary display of emotion?" She looked first at one and then at the other.

"My dear Amy," Ernst was the one to reply. He had regained his composure if not his self-confidence. "You must be aware that your son spent the whole of a holiday from school working with me in your kitchen garden at Templeton. We naturally became friends since we were companions in adversity."

"You may have been in adversity, Ernst. I concede that. But Rupert, surely not. He was in his own home, free as air to do whatever he pleased. He was under no obligation to work in the garden. I never forced him to do it. He chose to."

"No, you did not force me into the garden, Mother. But since you didn't organise any occupation for me in those dismal days there was little alternative."

"I'm sorry if I neglected you so shockingly during that impressionable age," she said caustically.

"I didn't mind in the end because Ernst was there. When he left I was miserable. I have been miserable without him ever since."

"Miserable? Miserable without him?" Amy questioned. She gave a forced little laugh. "You never told me that he meant anything to you then. You never told me that you missed him since. You never once mentioned his name."

For the first time Rupert brought himself to scrut-

inise his mother as he had scrutinised Ernst. The un-
bending, poker-faced, prudish, straight-laced woman
who would sit upright on the edge of chairs, declaiming
against the iniquities of the German race, was likewise
transformed. The woman in front of him, lolling on
a sofa with feet crossed, was somebody he did not
quickly recognise. Her face was heavily powdered,
her cheeks were rouged, her lips painted scarlet and
her hair, previously scooped back in a formidable bun,
was cut short at the nape of the neck. She was wearing a
gold and black silk taffeta dress, the skirt highly waisted
and tightly gathered around the calves of her legs in the
very latest fashion. The somewhat dowdy provincial
lady had been turned into, he was loth to admit it, an
attractive, if somewhat brassy flirt.

Amy went on: "Yes, Ernst, I can understand that
the two of you made friends in the garden, but what
is all this nonsense about the pledge and loving each
other for ever? And embracing each other too? Who
ever heard of such a thing between two men, or rather
a man and a boy?"

"Rupert is being a little hysterical after his long
journey, that is all, darling," Ernst answered, but the
flush across his cheeks contended with his airy manner
of brushing aside the charge. The airy manner and the
nonchalant *darling* stirred something in the depths of
Rupert's vitals. Ugly resentment began bubbling to
the surface like sediment in a cauldron.

At that moment a valve of the folding doors opened
noiselessly and a tiny boy dressed in a sailor suit with
a white lanyard and whistle round his open neck
was thrust by an invisible hand into the library.
The child hesitated on the threshold. "Maman!" it
said shyly. Straining his eyes Rupert recognised his
brother, Peregrine.

153

"Oh nurse!" Amy called out, "I'm afraid we're busy just at the moment. It isn't very convenient. Will you take him away." The child burst into tears and was hastily withdrawn.

Rupert gave a gasp. Suddenly the situation was made clear as day to him. An unexpected, squalid sequel to his and Ernst's noble relationship was revealed in a shaft of jaundiced illumination. He felt sick. He thought he would vomit. He did not know by which of the two people beside him he was more revolted.

"You ask what is all this nonsense about love between Ernst and me. Well, I shall tell you. Before you came on the scene—and I have no idea when that was—Ernst loved *me*. And because I loved him deeply, deeply, I allowed him to *make* love to me. Yes, *make* love, mother. That is something you can have no idea of. You who have loved only yourself, and had no affection either for Father or me. Do you suppose I did not realise that you were indifferent to Father all the time, while he was fighting in Flanders and the Near East? You can't suppose I was unaware of your total indifference to me also. Why, you were bored with me from the word go, bored to extinction. I was merely an encumbrance, something by which you did your duty like the chores at the hospital. You never cared for the patients, or the other nurses. You never made friends with any of them, or the neighbours. You merely hated the Germans. And Ernst is one. He taught me that you were wrong in making me hate them too. He changed all that. Then I felt sorry for him. And we made a solemn pledge, I tell you, sealed with a sacred kiss, such as you can never have exchanged with another person, male or female. I have the pledge in Ernst's own writing"—and he tapped the breast pocket of his flannel jacket—"I have it here. He wrote that I need

154

have no fear. He would always honour it. And that, if you want to know, is why I have come here today, to ask him to honour it. You, behind my back, have tried to come between us. You made him give you that brat, I presume. It wasn't Father's. And so Father turned you out of the house, isn't that true?"

"No, it is not true," Amy managed to interpolate. Rupert was so wound up that he could barely listen. He went on: "I don't believe you. Anyway I don't mind what you say. But I do mind what Ernst says." He was shouting.

Amy remained outwardly calm although she was seething within.

"Kindly shut up, you disgusting little beast!" she said. "I insist on being allowed to speak. Ernst, is it true what he says, that you actually kissed him, made love to him? It is the most disgraceful accusation I have ever heard. It passes my comprehension. It is like Oscar Wilde and that unmentionable Lord. To think that a child of mine can make such an insinuation, can actually boast of being a party to such a thing. Tell me it is all a pack of lies." She was addressing their host.

Ernst looked uncomfortable. He took a gulp, tossed back his head and through the slits of his falcon eyes pierced in turn first son, then mother. "I hope," he said with the utmost scorn, "never again to witness such a vulgar display of feelings."

"You may hope so. I hope so too," Amy rejoined. "But you haven't answered my question. Were you guilty of these filthy acts?"

"I am not accustomed to being cross-questioned in my own house," he said. "Nevertheless I consent to say this. Your son is grossly exaggerating. At first I disliked him because I thought him an insolent little cub. For weeks I would have nothing to do with him.

155

I would not speak to him. But he pressed his attentions on me. It was I who felt sorry for him. I realised he was lonely. I swallowed my pride and decided to make a friend of him since we were obliged to work closely together. But that I kissed him, and made love to him, as he claims, is pure fabrication. Ugh! the very idea is repellent to me." And he turned his face away from both of them.

"There! you are just inventing things out of spite," Amy addressed Rupert with ill-repressed venom. "You are insulting him." To Ernst she said with a sweet smile, "Sorry, darling, even for putting such a question to you. Please forgive me."

Rupert stood up. Ashen in the face he confronted Ernst. "Liar!" he screamed, "Judas! Liar! Judas!" Ignoring his mother he ran to the door, fumbled with the handle in his agony, and left the room. In the passage he could not remember the way he had come. He tried one door and then another. Before he reached the main staircase Ernst who had followed caught up with him. "Ruprecht!" he exclaimed, "kleiner Ruprecht, listen to me. Let me explain. Your mother . . . Don't run away, I beg. You can't leave like this. But you must grow up. We all have to grow up. I will make it right for you. Please, Ruprecht. I will always be your friend."

"Never," Rupert replied. And looking Ernst straight between the eyes, "I hate you. I shall always despise you." He wrenched himself free and darted down the stone stairs. He ran down the long vaulted corridor and, the back door being open, into the courtyard whence he came. He had a fleeting vision of the superior footman whose name was Gunther in a white apron and shirt sleeves, his bare brawny arms polishing a silver wine cistern engraved with a gigantic coronet. He did not stop to retrieve the yellow outfit although it was still raining. His bicycle was where he had left it, leaning against an outer column of the porte-cochère. The saddle was soaking wet. He took hold of the handle-bars, threw a flannelled leg over the seat and pedalled as hard as he could beyond the house and down the drive. The rain stung his eyes in his flight.

He was barely conscious of what he was doing. He did not know where he was going. He did not care. It did not matter. The scene he had just been through recurred to him in spasms, jerkily. The last incidents were the first, in rapid flashes. "Please, Ruprecht. I will always be your friend." Oh God, the cruelty of it. For the first time during the hellish interview Ernst's mask had dropped. He assumed that tender look Rupert remembered in the Temple of Flora. Truth and honour. Under Flora's broken nose. Flora knew, the harlot, what was to come. "You must grow up. We all have to grow up." It was sheer, unadulterated treachery. There was no other word for it. If to grow up meant treachery, then let him for ever remain a child. Kleiner Ruprecht, indeed. The man he had idealised for three years. Broken, shattered into a thousand fragments. "Liar! Judas!" Rupert was shouting the words into the wind and the rain. Christ, have mercy!

Down the drive he sped, skidding round the rutted corners, loose stones shooting from the front wheel. "You are just inventing out of spite. You are insulting him." *She* would never understand if she lived to be a thousand. But how could Ernst, how could he say, "Ugh! The very idea is repellent to me"? It was untrue. "The insolent little cub. Disgusting little beast." That horrid, puling little Peregrine too, begotten by Ernst on his mother. God might forgive him. He couldn't. "A little hysterical after his long

157

journey, my darling." His darling, that slick, smooth, cosmopolitan bounder's darling. It was nauseating. Who were they, these strangers? "Der Herr Graf will receive you in the library." They were nothing to do with him, nothing.

The castellated lodge came into view. The stone gate piers flew towards him. The spikes of the broken gates were raised like lances to tear his flesh, to enter his soul. Stop! He couldn't. It was too late. A terrible fear gripped him. A hay waggon laden to the billowing blue-grey sky. He pressed with both hands the brake levers. He back-pedalled. Automatically. It was useless. It didn't really matter. Nothing mattered. He wouldn't be frightened any more. It had to happen. It was even a mercy that one need no longer fear the future. One could just relax with one's golden memories. They alone were real.

The impact was so stupendous that he almost laughed. What was he doing? Soaring like a kite into the darkling air. He was fully conscious that he could fly at last. It was delicious. He had power, absolute power over good and evil. He could overcome the bitterest enemy. "Oh Ernst!" he was shouting again. "Look out for yourself, Ernst!"

(27)

Ernst and Amy were sitting side by side at a small table with thick black legs and a thick black polished top in a corner of the *herrenzimmer* at Schloss Ehrenberg. In the centre of the table glimmered a too intricately chased silver statuette of a mounted knight in armour upon

158

an ebony plinth. Upon the plinth were engraved in Gothic runes the name of the equestrian hero and some lines of an elegy calculated to remind the observer of Germany's glorious medieval past. The walls of the room were lined with long and narrow black-varnished panels of the same funereal wood as the plinth. All of a sudden a gleam of horizontal sunshine cast a feint of light, not naturally golden, but unnaturally puce, through the opaque pane of a stained glass window as though to make amends for the deplorable weather of the morning and afternoon. The shaft shot like an arrow of doom across the white Saxony dinner plate, relieved by a painted escutcheon and coronet, which Amy's slender fingers were fondling for warmth. From an obscure corner of the room a clock intoned eight well-spaced, deep booms. Amy gave a gentle sigh as of gratitude for this mechanical interruption of the heavy silence. She interpreted it as a signal of redemption from the intensely disagreeable scene in the library. Since Gunther and the second footman were momentarily out of the room fetching the meat course Amy ventured to put her left hand caressingly on Ernst's right arm. He made no shift either to return her pressure or to withdraw his arm.

"Let's try to forget Rupert's intolerable behaviour, shall we, darling?" she asked. "The odious boy."

Before Ernst could express agreement or disagreement Gunther returned alone through the varnished door which separated dining-room from serving-room. He carried no dish and approached Ernst's chair with deliberate footsteps.

"Herr Graf," he announced gravely, "they have sent word from the lodge that there has been an accident on the main road just outside the gates."

"What sort of an accident, Gunther?" Ernst asked

with apparent unconcern.

"It seems that an hour or so ago a haywain collided with a man on a velocipede. The lodge-keeper was obliged to take in the injured man. His wife attended to him while the doctor was sent for."

"Good God, man, why didn't you tell me before?" Ernst's face was suddenly tautened with anxiety as he rose to his feet.

"Because I did not think fit to interrupt your Highness's dinner before the doctor arrived. It now seems that the man was calling Your Highness's name. And the doctor insisted that Your Highness should be informed."

"Damnation take you!" Ernst shouted as he threw his napkin on the floor. "Is the man still in the lodge, or has he been taken to the hospital?"

"In the lodge. I understand it's too late to take him to the hospital," Gunther imparted this piece of information with the self-satisfaction that a well-trained servant communicates the worst possible news. His face was as serene and expressionless as an undertaker's.

Without further hesitation Ernst sprang to the door and without a word to Amy ran down the passage to the hall, seized a stalking cap from a miscellaneous collection on the rack made of deers' antlers, crammed it on his head and rushed through the front door and down the drive. Within twenty minutes he had reached the lodge, breathless. Under the little porch stood the local doctor in a black frock coat, a stethoscope hanging from his neck, a neat gladstone bag in his left hand.

"I hope Your Highness will think I did right," he said, while doffing his black trilby hat deferentially, "since the poor young man seemed in his extremity to be calling Your Highness's first name." And he bowed stiffly in anticipation of pardon for the liberty he was taking by the suggestion that Count Detmold-Ehrenberg had acquaintances among the lesser orders of mankind. To this presumption Ernst paid no heed and, without looking at the dignified figure before him, said brusquely, "Tell me, Herr Doktor, is he alive?"

"He is dead, Your Highness. No one could have survived the head fractures he sustained," the doctor replied in a voice as respectful as it was devoid of grief. "How many such cases have I not encountered of boys riding these dreadful, unreliable two-wheelers. Dear me, dear me!" And stepping aside he added, "I assume that, although this lamentable accident took place at Your Highness's gate it is in order for me to have the remains collected and taken to the Brandenburg mortuary at the public expense, until the relatives of the deceased can be traced, and their wishes made known as to internment."

"Do no such thing," Ernst commanded severely, "and please wait, Herr Doktor, a minute." He brushed past him into the small living room of the lodge. The glow from a single candle, piously stuck in an old beer bottle by the lodge-keeper's wife, did nothing to dispel the darkness. The symbol of peasant homage to death merely dazzled Ernst's eyes. He removed it. A dull trickle of daylight filtered through the lattice panes upon the outline of a figure spread on the lodge-keeper's couch. A blanket had been thrown over the body and the face was already covered by a cloth. Without a pretence of reverence Ernst snatched off the cloth. Recognising at a glance Rupert's bruised and mutilated features he hastily recovered them. The lodge-keeper's wife was standing at a discreet distance. She held a handkerchief to her eyes, endeavouring not to shed tears.

161

"Thank you, Frau Hebbel," he said to the woman. "It has been a shock to you. I am sorry. You have been a good Samaritan. You have behaved correctly and kindly. I will have him removed to the castle as soon as possible." He was surprised by the control of his own voice. He took hold of the woman's hand and said gently, "Do not be ashamed. You do well to weep for him."

"So young, Eure Durchlaucht," she murmured.

Ernst left the lodge by the porch where the doctor was waiting.

"Yes, the young man was a friend of mine. I will be responsible for him and let you know what steps I want taken when I receive his parents' wishes. Meanwhile may I ask you to engage a nurse and the undertaker. Good evening, Herr Doktor."

"Guten abend, Eure Durchlaucht."

Slowly Ernst climbed the hill. He was in no hurry. He had no need to ponder. He knew what he must do. He went straight to the library where Amy was crouching before the flickering fire. She raised a mildly enquiring face which showed not a trace of anxiety.

"Well, what was it?" She spoke in the tone of a bored wife asking a husband on his return from hunting what sport he had had, a tone which at the time of utterance she little realised was to forfeit all her happiness in the years that remained to her.

"It," Ernst replied savagely, "was your son. That's all. That is what it was."

"Oh!" came from Amy in a very little cry, short and clipped as if she had unexpectedly pricked a finger on a hidden pin in her blouse and did not want to make too much fuss about it. "It was Rupert then. Oh goodness! How dreadful, isn't it?" Ernst made no reply to the prosaic interrogation and left the room. He rang

162

bells, issued orders and acted with automatic precision and efficiency. The chauffeur, summoned from his quarters, drove him down to the lodge. With his help and that of the lodge-keeper Ernst lifted Rupert's loose body into the back seat of the motor. He sat beside it letting the lifeless head fall upon his shoulder. Ernst himself carried the body upstairs and laid it gently on a bed which he had ordered to be prepared in a bedroom next to his. He went down to the library where Amy was still sitting, hunched and gazing into the fading embers.

"Amy," he said, "should you not send a cable at once to Rupert's father? Perhaps you should go upstairs and see him first, just to assure yourself, you know."

"Yes," she replied, "perhaps I had better."

She went upstairs and within a few minutes came down, absolutely dry-eyed, and holding a sheet of writing-paper. "This is what I suggest should be sent to Joshua. Can you have it dispatched for me, Ernst."

"Of course, it shall be done at once," he said.

(28)

The servants' hall at Templeton Manor was a much jollier room than it used to be. The younger maids had even dared to paste on the walls photographs, torn out of the *Tatler* and other magazines, of their pin-up boys—Douglas Fairbanks, then starring in *The Thief of Baghdad*, Ivor Novello at the piano actually playing and singing his own composition, *Keep the Home Fires Burning*, and, more popular still, Rudolph Valentino as Julio in that highly romantic silent film, *The Four Horses of the Apocalypse*. Pritchard didn't know what things were coming to, she didn't. Things were never like that in the old Squire's day, nor even in the late mistress's.

"Is she dead then?" asked the new kitchen-maid (all the servants engaged since November 1918 and even those who had worked in the house before the war and been re-engaged, were referred to as "new").

"No, she isn't—exactly," Pritchard answered.

"Which means she is alive then," observed the youngest of the new housemaids.

"She may be alive to some people, but not to us," Pritchard hissed. This remark should have clinched the matter had the new kitchen-maid possessed delicacy, an attribute in which she was signally lacking. "Not since she were screwed by that Jerry, I s'pose," she said.

There was a really dreadful pause, more pregnant with heavy breathing on the part of Pritchard and Mrs Staples, than silence. Presently the former spoke:

"Go upstairs this instant, Nellie. And don't leave your room again today. You won't have no supper. That I should live to hear such an expression in this hall beats the band. Things has come to a pretty pass these days. It's the war 'as done it. Where can the girl have been edicated?" Like a thunder cloud she looked down upon the others.

"Not edicated," observed Mrs Staples who, always a trifle behind-hand in her reactions, now threw her apron over her face and indulged in mouse-like screeches of horror.

"The missus was a lady," Pritchard hastened to assure the others, "and whatever ladies does is different to you coarse-grained creatures."

The rebuke was enough to dismiss from the hall those young girls who had not already followed Nellie. The two old cronies were left, each with her feet on the fender before the empty grate, for it was early September. The rapid click of Pritchard's steel knitting-needles might have suggested to Turkish ears the stropping of scimitars for an execution in the Seraglio; the slower upward and downward heave of Mrs Staples's bone crochet-hook the action of a Newgate hangman striving to hoist his victim into the noose.

"Of course they doesn't know the worst," Pritchard resumed when they were alone.

Mrs Staples looked up. "About—" she began and thought better of continuance.

"Master Peregrine," Pritchard finished the sentence for her.

Mrs Staples's nod could be interpreted that either that was what she meant to say, or what she did not mean to say.

"I have never let on, never, although contrary to what the missus believes. She has always held it against me, I know. And unless the master himself has told others, how did that little hussey get to hear of such a thing? Even Master Rupert don't know. I wouldn't for the world he did neither. But you see, Elsie (this was the first time in very many years Pritchard had condescended to use the cook's Christian name; it portended a deep confidence), I worries about that boy. Between you and me and the gate post I knows where he's gone to. Just mark my words."

"What words?" Mrs Staples had the spirit to enquire.

"I'm coming to them," Pritchard said rather testily. "You be always in such a hurry, Mrs Staples." This back-hander, coupled with the reversion to the cook's title and surname, was an indication of the parlour-maid's slight displeasure. "Now you've put me out. What was I a-saying?"

"Words," Mrs Staples reminded her.

"Oh yes. The boy's gone to Germany, I'll be bound. And to see that Ernest too."

"Never!" exclaimed her companion.

"I said he's gone to see that Ernest. And what I says I means. What's more, he'll not come back once he gets there." Pritchard's lower lip began to tremble.

"Deary, deary me!" Mrs Staples exclaimed.

"He's bewitched. That's what he is. He's never been the same since he worked in the kitchen garden those Easter holidays, nigh three and a half years ago. That Ernest is a wizard to my way o' thinking. And no better than he ought to be."

"But Sam," Mrs Staples began, only to cut herself short with a snap of her dentures for no apparent reason.

"Brother Sam's a fool. He's no more judge of a man than this ball of wool. The Kaiser's only to smile for him to fall flat on his face."

There was a timid knock. One of the housemaids put her head round the door. "If you please, Mrs Staples," she said while putting her finger to her lips so that Pritchard, whose back was turned to the door, should not see.

Mrs Staples rose painfully. Painfully she waddled to the door, passed through and closed it behind her.

"What is it?" she asked.

"It's a cable come from the Post Office. The telegraph boy brought it special. 'E says it's bad news. I thought I'd best 'and it to you seeing as how Miss Pritchard might take on. And should you forward it to the Squire in Scotland? Thank you, Mrs Staples."

The cook did not open it. She knew her place in the hierarchy. She would not presume to trespass upon the parlour-maid's prerogative however distressing these might be for her friend. She went back into the servants' hall, closing the door again and working her way to her chair. Slowly she sat down.

"A telegram," she said, handing the buff envelope to Pritchard.

"A telegram seldom brings nobody any good," Pritchard said, fumbling for the string of her pince-nez which had got caught in a button of her blouse. "But perhaps's the Squire's coming home sooner than expected, and without one of them fluffs and tinsels I don't think."

She opened the envelope. "Oh dear, it's from abroad." Then she read: "Fiennes-Templeton, Templeton Manor, near Stafford, England. Deeply distressed inform you darling little Rupert bicycle accident died peacefully love Amy."

"There, what did I tell you, Elsie? No, no, I can't bear it. I can't." She did not cry. Yet the tears chose of their own accord to flow in a steady course down her apple cheeks, without a muscle of her rugged face moving.

Mrs Staples was likewise dreadfully concerned. With an effort she got out of her chair, moved across to her companion in distress and put both hands on her shoulders.

"There, there, Olive. It's all right, dear." It was just about the longest speech anyone had ever heard her make. And it had the effect of arousing in Pritchard her old fire.

"It's *not* all right. It's all *wrong*, Mrs Staples," she said with heavy emphasis.

"All wrong," Mrs Staples reiterated.

(29)

While, on the following morning, a woman from the village did her grisly business with the corpse and two black-suited men took measurements for a coffin, Amy in the library awaited a reply from Joshua. Ernst stayed apart in his little study. They met for lunch but there seemed little to say. By the evening a cable from her ex-husband was received. It read, "Devastated. Do what you think proper as to funeral. I shall not criticise. Deep sympathy. Joshua." And the cable bore the name of a remote post office in the Outer Hebrides. There was no suggestion that his son's body ought to be brought home to Templeton for burial, and no indication that he intended to join her in Germany.

When Amy handed the buff sheet of paper to Ernst he exploded with indignation. "Hast der Mann kein Herz?" he exclaimed. "Can neither of you spare either compassion or one tear? What is the matter with you English people? Are you eaten up with self-esteem? Is grief an emotion you are too exalted, too proud to show? Are you ashamed of loving? Is that it? Yes, little Rupert was right. You deprived that sensitive child of affection. All his troubles derived from that single factor. Now I understand. You are ashamed of love. You are stiff-necked and cold. Vous me faites horreur," he hissed the words. "As for me, I am ashamed of myself. I do not mind admitting it. I rejected him, poor little boy. I am to blame. I am as much responsible for his death as you. I repeat, I am abject with shame." And he covered his face with his hands.

Amy remained impassive. She did not speak and she could not cry although she felt her inability to summon tears was reprehensible. Her honesty proved stronger than her sense of decorum. From outside herself she

168

viewed the extraordinary situation. Here was this foreigner, her lover, moved to unnatural emotion by the sudden death of her son by another man, her son whom but yesterday both of them had rebuffed from the door. She had had no compunction. She could not reverse her sentiments overnight. Why therefore should he? What had their relationship amounted to, Ernst's and Rupert's? In spite of Ernst's denials and because of Rupert's wild protestations in this very room only twenty-four hours ago, there must have been some liaison between them. Her thoughts were interrupted by Ernst standing before her with a look of awesome resolution.

"I decide," he said. "Rupert shall be buried here, in my family vault, in my chapel in the park. I at any rate shall keep his body close to me. That is settled. You may tell his father what I intend to do if you like. That is your concern. I have made up my mind." And he pierced Amy through and through with the fire from his deep hawk's eyes. Amy quailed before his resolution. Had she wished, she dared not argue.

And so Rupert was buried according to the Calvinist rites within a small enclosure on the west side of a little Gothic chapel between the garden and park of the Castle of Ehrenberg. Sheep would graze within a few feet of his remains and cattle on summer evenings rub their matted flanks against the posts and rails that protected the consecrated enclosure. On winter evenings the wild deer seeking fodder would cast their shadows upon his grave.

When all was over Ernst lapsed into a condition of apparent inanition. He seldom spoke; he did not read. For the greater part of the day he remained in his little study which neither Amy nor the household cared to penetrate. Amy was not a sensitive woman, but even

169

she soon realised that it would be a mistake to prolong her visit to the term that had been agreed upon before she came. What she minded most was Ernst's total indifference, since Rupert's death, to the existence of Peregrine. It was even worse than his revulsion for her. She thought them both unjustifiable and inexplicable.

Ernst did not ask Amy to leave. She took the decision herself. At lunch three days after the funeral she announced that in the circumstances she would return to England. To her chagrin Ernst did not demur. On the contrary he agreed that it was suitable. The following morning the Count, gentlemanly to the last, went with Mrs Fiennes-Templeton, the nurse and baby Peregrine in the pre-war Hotchkiss to Berlin. He accompanied the little party to the platform of the Friedrichsstrasse station, found for them their reserved carriage, saw that the luggage was neatly stacked on the rack, and tipped the porter. With that innate or assumed courtesy which he displayed to man, woman and child of every degree, Ernst took off his hat, held it in his left hand and without a word or show of intimacy, far less of affection, raised Amy's gloved hand to his lips, shook the hand of the nurse, nodded to Peregrine, turned and walked, without once looking round, along the platform and out of sight. Amy was too stupefied to speak. She knew two things: that she had never mattered to him at all, and that she would never see him again.